Ways of the Native

By David Evans

Table of Contents

Chapter 1: Intro

While the West was still wild, there were over 574 Nations of Native American tribes. Each tribe believed in more than one God, which is similar to the beliefs of the Egyptians.

The natives believe that our planet is a living thing and that it must be respected, or destruction will surely follow. They openly talked to Mother Earth during their daily chants.

They would build sweat lodges; they would sit in the lodges together and would begin by pouring boiling water over the rocks, this would create steam.

The steam takes the impurities out of the body through sweating. They believe that everything living on Earth has its own vibration meaning everything releases a different frequency.

From a single celled organism to the largest animal on Earth. The natives relied on their Medicine Man to treat any dieses that they may encounter.

The native Americans used to harvest honey from the wild beehives using smoke and would crack open the hive and take out the honey.

Honeybees were brought to America from Europeans in the 16th century. In the 18th century the first bee box was constructed.

Sadly in 1770, 11,000 natives were killed off by the smallpox epidemic that was spread on their blankets, by people with an agenda to decimate their very existence. If that wasn't bad enough, the natives would soon find themselves forced to live on reservations. After the land they used to live on was taken away from them.

Tribes that didn't get along with one another were thrown together on the preserves, this only crippled their ability to sustain life.

They couldn't fight back or were beaten and even shot by the calvary. The natives were forced to go on death walks, one of these walks was called "The Trail of Tears."

This began in 1830 and ended in 1840, 100,000 Natives were forced from their homes.

The Indians were in chains with little to no food to eat. There didn't seem to be much recourse for the people who were doing this to them.

Native Americans weren't allowed to live where the settlers did. In 1785 Georgia, was where the first treaty was signed beginning the brutal ousting of the natives off of their land.

The nation was still young but still had a government that was beginning to show its brutal powers to destroy the lives of millions that it didn't like or understand.

The government soon drafted a document and came out with the Treaty of Hopewell, this treaty allowed the government to draw up the boundaries for the natives land.

Unfortunately, in 1791 the Cherokee were forced to give up the land just outside of their boundaries.

The Indians were now locked into a long-drawn-out battle for their very existence. On September 17, 1787, the Federal government was created with an intricate system of checks and balances.

The Federal government encouraged the Indians to leave their religious ways behind and become Christians, then told them to become farmers.

The Indians, who were hunters, struggled to learn the few farming techniques. The Indians weren't able to afford the supplies needed to compete a harvest. This caused some of the hunters to die from starvation.

If that wasn't hard enough on them they were forced to wear non-Indian clothes and to read and write and sewing techniques along with learning to raise livestock.

The Indians weren't allowed to leave the reservations without permission. After the Indians rigorously fought for their independent against Andrew Jacksons militia and lost.

This battle was called the battle of Horseshoe Bend, because of this defeat they lost 20 million acres of land to the Federal government.

This still wasn't enough for the government; they passed several acts to control the natives furthermore.

Before the acts were put into law the Cherokee were working on creating a new constitution that was their own government.

The Federal government didn't like having any kind of competition, once they caught wind of this ordered a seizure of the remaining Cherokee land in their state in December 1828.

The Indian Appropriations Act was passed by Congress in 1851, officially creating the Indian reservation system.

One year before the Indians were placed on reserves, chief Dyami was talking to Esadowa about a vision he had while he was in the sweat lodge a few hours ago.

In the vision I saw the great buffalo running across the plains, where it was met by a wolf and bear.

Then a hawk flew overhead, the bear stood up letting out a roar. The bear and the wolf began fighting fiercely among themselves, then I heard thunder in the distance and the bear and wolf suddenly disappeared.

Then militia men showed up and began beating on the bison, until it's body could no longer survive the punishment and it collapsed.

Then the land that they were standing on began to crack apart and they lost their balance falling down into the Earth. Their bodies were engulfed in red flames and disappeared.

"Was that the end of your vision?"

"Yes."

"What did the red flames represent?"

"Evil."

"What about the wolf and bear?"

"Coming Conflict."

For the past three days I've been having these visions.

"Have you mentioned these visions to anyone besides me?"

"Yes."

I mentioned it to the medicine man, and it left him alarmed. In the coming days I'll be spending time with the elders of the Shawnee tribe.

"Can I go with you?"

"No."

"Are you going to come along with me on my hunt later?"

"Yes."

Mother Earth is telling me that this evening we need to pray. I can sense the presence of the mighty eagle, he's somewhere close by.

Sometimes I have dreams that I'm a hawk flying across the sky. You have taught me so much in my life, you bring out my curiosity. Dyami stood up and exited the teepee.

"Where are you going?"

"To check on the sick child, he's been sick for days."

Chapter 2: Ready & Able

The child's mother has been talking to the Medicine Man daily. Sahale came running over to him, while I was out scouting for buffalo the four of us were attacked by a hostile tribesman.

"How many of them were there?"

"Two of them."

We killed them because we didn't want them to come back here and harm anyone.

You must get there rancid blood off of yourself, or evil entities will come after you. Cleanse yourself off in the river, while saying the peace chant.

I haven't saw your brother in a while, he's been busy out exploring. When he gets back here tell him to watch out for the evil ones.

Out of nowhere a cowboy riding a horse went galloping through their village, how dare he go through here like that. If I had more energy I'd be chasing after him right now.

You shouldn't associate yourself with him, he's nothing but trouble. Gunfire erupted nearby; they don't seem to care who they shoot at.

"Why are you checking on this boy?"

"Because he's sick and I want to learn from the Medicine Man."

Sahale lost interest and walled off, while Esadowa stayed around observing the medicine man. The Medicine Man was burning sage and sweet grass.

"Why are you burning a combination of sage and sweet grass?"

"It helps to cure the boys mind of any evil."

The wind began to pick up and blew out the sage and sweet grass. I can sense that there's some evil around at the moment.

The Medicine Man broke out in chant, with his eyes closed. Meanwhile in Pennsylvania the Shawnee were fighting off the remaining hostile attackers from another tribe.

The tribe that attacked them, are called the sworkerts. These have known to be a bully to many tribes.

Two sworkert warriors rode away on their horses, but a Shawnee warrior named Sixsipita quickly went after them and soon caught up with them.

He shot an arrow into one of their backs, causing him to fall down from his horse. The second warrior swung his ax at him, but he ducted and took off after him again.

The enemy warriors horse slide down a muddy embankment, the warrior was thrown down abruptly and dislocated his shoulder.

Sixsipita stayed back from the embankment, he got off his horse and grabbed his bow and an arrow.

He placed the arrow in his bow and pulled it back, while aiming it at the enemy and let go of the strings. The arrow went into the chest of the enemy, and he collapsed.

Tasunke rode up behind Sixsipita, I've never seen you ride so fast. You have to settle yourself and get down next to me right now or you'll get us both seen by the enemy spy who's coming this way.

"Are we going to have to fight him?"

"He whispered no."

A crow flew overhead and landed in a nearby tree and began to squawk, the spy looked their way and saw the horses then looked away and continued what he was doing. Don't talk, stay quiet we'll keep observing him. Don't let your horse move, or the spy may come over here. The spy was now out of view, I'm glad that he's gone.

I think we should have killed him, but I know you'll disagree with me. We have done enough killing, Mother Earth wouldn't us killing any more today. They came to a patch of sweet grass; I love the smell of sweet grass.

"Why don't you pick some?"

"No."

I remember when your brother trained that hawk to land on his arm.

"Whatever happened to that hawk?"

"It just disappeared."

"Why was your brother ousted from our tribe?"

"I'm not sure."

"Why don't you get on your horse?"

"I sense danger."

There may be an ambush waiting for us, and for now we need to stay behind the trees to stay hidden.

Four militia men were galloping across the meadow, hopefully they don't us up here. My senses are always heightened, and you must work on your senses.

"Do you think those men are going to attack our village?"

"No," there looking for someone.

"Whom do you think there after?"

"An outlaw."

There's a man coming our way with a gun, we don't want no trouble here. I know your kind, your Shawnee Indians.

Those militia men are looking for me, and I have no place to go to escape. I don't want you thinking I'm going to let you both go.

Give me whatever you have of value and do it quickly. The man pulled the hammer back and pushed the barrel into Sixsipita's forehead, if your pal tries anything I'll shoot.

"What's he reaching for in the saddle?"

"A knife to give to you."

I'm not interested in a knife; you're wasting my time. Once the militia came closer the man he hid behind Sixsipita, the militia men shouted out step away from the Indian.

The man shouted I will not, you'll have to shoot me. The militia began to talk among themselves, we should just shoot him.

This is the second time he's escaped the county jail. He's murdered someone already and you need to end his reign, he's also a thief.

Start shooting when I say to, you're being a fool you murderer. I know what I'm doing, let's get this over with.

The leader of the militia shouted shoot, and all four men began firing at will. The murder got shot in the shoulder and ducked behind a tree.

Both Shawnee Indians also took cover, the murderer was in intense pain and struggled to shoot his weapon.

One of the militia men fired his colt revolver and the bullet hit the murder in the head, instantly killing him. The militia men came over to the Indians, it's okay now you're free to go.

"Are you going to harm us?"

"No."

"What's the knife doing on the ground?"

"The man threw it on the ground."

Don’t worry about the body we’ll take care of it. Go ahead go, get on your horses. They got on their horses and took off over to the creek, I don’t know about you, but my ears are still ringing.

Chapter 3: Lesson

Mother Earth became disrupted with all that mindless gun fire. Civilized people don't know about Mother Earth and nor do they want to help her very often.

They let their brass from the bullets lay back there, brass can seep into Mother Earths soil and hurt her.

That's why I shoot a bow and shoot arrows. The settlers are ruining our once pristine bodies of water by their livestock and stagecoaches crossing the river.

This creek used to be a nice to go to relax, now there's things in it that shouldn't be. Mother Earth doesn't want you to worry yourself, she says that you need to get back to you.

The sun God is sending his blessings onto us today with the warmth of life. The ground has become dry and once healthy plants are now withering away and the rain God hasn't called for rain.

You should pray to the rain God; shall we start praying here. No, we really should get back to our village, we must keep our people safe.

"Why do you have your ear to the ground?"

"I can feel the vibration of cattle coming this way."

It's probably a herd of bison, coming here to graze on the grass. They got on their horses and galloped along the creek.

Our village is low on their supply of fish, this area of the creek isn't deep enough to find fish. Your father used to amaze me how he would sometimes catch the trout with his bare hands.

"Did he teach you how to do that?"

"No," he passed away before he could.

"What do you see?"

"Fox tracks."

"Do you want to hunt for the fox?"

"No," and these are old tracks.

"Do you know who this is coming our way?"

"He's a trapper and a good friend of mine."

"Hello good friend what brings you

out today?"

"I'm checking my traps."

"Did you get the elusive fox?"

"No."

The beaver sure have been plentiful this year, I've caught dozens of them. I haven't seen you in town very often lately. I'd rather stay out in the wilderness where I belong.

"How's your son doing?"

"He's doing well."

I can't seem to get this trap to open to set it, I'd help you, but I don't want to ruin your trap. It takes a lot to ruin one of these traps.

I could teach you how to hunt vermin without using these traps. We use six kinds of primitive traps and use a different trap depending on what kind of animal it is. I prefer to use a snare trap; I find what you're saying to be rather interesting.

"How many of these traps do you set in a day?"

"Four of them."

"Have you ever set fish traps?"

"No." I don't like to eat fish, but my wife does.

"What do you call a fish trap?"

"It's called a funnel trap."

"Are those traps difficult to set up?"

"No," you use the lay of the land to your advantage.

You must direct the fish to your trap, it's simple to do. You can use stones or sticks to set up the trap, pile up stones around where the fish are.

Then you strike the fish with a spear or net them. You summed that up well, I'll give it a try.

My cousin wants to learn the ways of the Indian, I'll have to take him out here with me sometime. We better be on our way, they waved goodbye as they rode off.

Soon they came to field with tall grass, this is where my other horse got bitten by a rattle snake.

My great grandfather told me to watch out for snakes, he used to say the devil would spawn snakes to test us.

That sounds like an odd tall tale to me. I didn't believe everything that he spoke, but that tale stuck with me. We should do some trading today at the trade post.

"What do you need from there?"

"Some deer hide."

My shirt is torn, my wife could fix that for you. There's no need to do that, I'll fix it for you.

Suddenly they heard gunfire nearby, they galloped as quickly as possible and eventually came to their village and luckily all was well.

Back to Chief Dyami, the Medicine Man finished his chants and the sick boy fell asleep with his mother beside him.

His mother knew that her son was safe with the Medicine Man and chief Dyami, so she walked out of the teepee and was going to tend to her chores.

Suddenly a rabid fox came running out of the woods and began trying to bite a villager.

The chief sensed that something wasn't right and got up and ran towards the threat.

He attacked the rabid fox with his tomahawk, killing it with one blow to the head.

He picked up its dead body and threw it into the campfire. An Indian approached him and said I can feel the demon spirit among us.

"Where are you going Chief?"

"To the sacred creek to wash the tainted blood off my hands."

Once at the creek he did a scared spirit ritual, a fawn came to the creek. He found this to be alarming, before he was about to let out a word the deer turned to black smoke and disappeared.

After seeing the evil, he began to chant. Chills went down his back and after quite some time the evil left the area, and the land was calm again.

He left the sacred creek and went back to his teepee to rest. A few months later the militia was sent out by the Federal government, to survey the land and begin working on setting up the land boundaries. Dyami stood his ground and stood up to the militia men.

If you don't get back from us, were going to do something you're not going to like. Then Dyami walked away from the men, we'll be out of here.

Another Indian came over, trying to understand what the men were saying and doing.

You Indians don't need to know what we're doing here, I'm going to push you back soon.

Chapter 4: Big Bear

This is our land said the Indian, no it's not said one of the men in an authoritative voice. You won't have your own land when we're done.

This only angered the Indian, he shouted a war call to his people who then came over to him. There are more than us than you, you're just a mumbling fool.

We have guns and aren't afraid to use them. This confrontation went on until the Indians fought with the militia men. From there things rapidly escalated and treaties and laws were set in place.

Dyami's last words were you'll never be able to confine my soul, I'm a free spirit. The Shawnee tribe wasn't able to hold out and went down with the other tribes.

Part 2:

There was an Indian chief, and his name was chief Big Bear, he had big muscular arms and wore a head dress. His cloths were made out of deer hide and he lived in South Dakota.

He was a good hunter and could sneak up on any animal, his brother's name was Keeko. Keeko was five years younger than him, he was twenty-four years old.

Big Bear and Keeko would always go hunting together, they were both in charge of gathering food for their tribe.

On some of their hunts they would come in contact with dangerous wildlife. One day Keeko went missing, Chief Big Bear was upset that he didn't sleep for two nights, he had a beautiful wife. Her name was Lena, she had beautiful long hair that was shoulder length.

Big Bear would talk to Lena about Keeko, Lena loved to spend time with Big Bears brother.

Every afternoon she would wash up in the river. She wouldn't get entirely naked; she would always wear deer hide over her particular body parts.

He would always protect Lena, one time a rattle snake was crawling towards Lena while she was asleep.

He quickly pulled out his knife and hit the snake twice with the knife. The snake stopped moving and he lifted up the snake and threw it into the fire pit.

He had a large tee pee, in the center of the tee pee was a small fire which kept them warm. There were small rocks all around the fire pit.

These small rocks were from the creek, these rocks were slippery and didn't have many rough edges.

He always had plenty of blankets to keep himself covered with; his great grandmother sewed the blankets.

Lena liked to play the flute, she would play the flute each morning for an hour or two, and this would relax her mind.

The sound from the flute would easily cause big bear to fall back asleep and that's exactly what he was going to.

Big Bear and Lena wouldn't sleep directly on the ground. But instead, he made a special matt out of deer skin.

It was better than sleeping on the ground, he went into a dream. The dream only lasted for a short while; he couldn't remember what he had dreamt about.

The dream had left his mind, he kept a lot of sage inside of the tee pee. He sometimes would burn the sage grass when he would have a special gathering. He just recently had a special ceremony, he had two children with Lena.

His children were always in good health, they learned quickly how to hunt and gather food for the tribe. When his children were just fourteen years old he taught them how to track and hunt buffalo. They quickly became good skilled hunters; his children were now on their own and we're no longer with big bear. His children moved away from him and we're living in the tribe that was next to him.

Lena wore moccasins, they were made of buffalo hide. They always kept her feet warm; she wore a necklace with amethyst crystals on it.

She would make the meals for the tribe; she enjoyed cooking and would take her time and make a good fresh meal.

One-day Big Bear and Keeko came back from a buffalo hunt, they had a lot of meat hanging around their body. They brought the meat to Lena, and she cooked the meat over the open fire.

Lena would cook the meat for just a few minutes then take it off of the open flame. Lena and big bear and Keeko would sit by the fire and enjoy their dinner together. Lena would cook every night except for rare occasions.

He wasn't a good cook, one time he was cooking, and the piece of buffalo meat fell into the open flame of the fire, and he couldn't get it out.

That piece of meat turned black, and nobody could eat it. He didn't like to waste buffalo meat.

He would take as much as he could before leaving the head of the buffalo behind. He would use every part of the buffalo, except for its head. He would use the horns of the buffalo to store his gun powder. Big Bear didn't have much gun powder and had just two muzzle loaders. These muzzle loaders were for him and Lena.

His brother Keeko preferred to use his long bow and didn't like to use a gun to kill anything.

He would say that he liked to use pure instinct when he was hunting. He didn't like the loud bang and smoke that the muzzle loader would make.

All of his life he would use a long bow to go hunting with. He liked to use the muzzle loader for hunting the buffalo.

He would get the black powder from civilized man; he would often trade goods with the local town folk.

He would get along good with the civilized man he met a known mountain man one time.

His name was Robert. Big Bear will never forget him because he was kind to him, he was never lonely.

He always had Lena by his side, it would take him half of the day just to come back from hunting buffalo with Keeko.

He would cut up the buffalo with his sharp knife, it would take him awhile to entirely skin a buffalo. The last trade that he made with the civilized man was me buffalo meat for a set of binoculars.

These binoculars always came in handy for him. He could look ahead at the buffalo heard and look for the most mature buffalo and that's the one he would

Chapter 5: Keeko

harvest. Big Bear wouldn't kill an animal and let it lay, he knew that each time he would hunt a buffalo he was putting himself and his brother Keeko at risk of getting trampled.

Big bear and Keeko have never been trampled by a buffalo. They have been lucky.

The herd of buffalo was large, there were about twenty of them in a herd. The mature Bulls would be on the outside of the herd, while the young buffalo were in the middle of the heard which gave them protection from the predators.

He would never just kill a young buffalo. One-time Keeko missed a mature bull buffalo, and his arrow struck a young buffalo. It took three arrows to finish off the young buffalo, big bear scolded Keeko and said what's the matter with you. You know that you shouldn't kill a young buffalo. His brother replied it wasn't my fault.

My arrow missed the mature bull and hit the young buffalo. Don't let it happen again or I won't let you go hunting with me anymore. Big Bear had five beautiful horses

He wouldn't ride them every day, each horse looked different. One of the horses was white with a few brown spots on its back.

It had a brown spot near its left eye, the other horse was all black except for a white spot on its left shoulder.

The horses were three or four years old. Big bear only had these five horses for a year or so.

He would take good care of them and make sure he would take all five horses to the creek twice a day they could have a drink of fresh water.

One time when he took the five horses to the creek, the black horse tried to run away.

Luckily he was able to chase the horse down only after a few minutes of chasing him. The four horses just watched big bear catch the five horse, he was almost out of breath.

He gently petted the black horse, he said to him why must you always run away on me? Continued on petting the side of head.

The black horses name was stalker. Big bear didn't name this horse, Keeko did. Big Bear couldn't understand why Keeko named the horse this name.

He never asked Keeko why. It was changing seasons, from winter to spring. The temperature was on the cool side, it was about fifty-five degrees outside.

He prefers the warmer weather. On hot sunny days in the summertime, he likes to lay out in the grassy field and look up into the sky.

His wife Lena prefers the wintertime, she likes to see it snow. When it snows big bear and Lena stay in their tee pee. The five horses stay right outside of the tee pee.

They never wander far from Big Bears tee pee, one of the horses is shorter than the rest of them. Keeko named it tiny. He didn't like this name and one day is going to rename the horse.

He was always feeling sad since Keeko went missing two days ago, he was spending me time with the other neighboring tribe. When the space people came down and took them away.

He was going to figure out a way to fight back against the space people. He and his wife Lena were going to have to fight the space people.

Big Bear is a quiet soul that doesn't like to fight, his wife doesn't like to fight either. Big bear was feeling like going on an adventure today. He woke up and looked over at Lena, Lena was still asleep. She was facing away from him.

He felt her arm and it felt cold, he took an extra blanket and placed it over her arm. This must have disturbed her, she awoke and rolled over and now was facing big bear. She asked what's the matter? I'm feeling like going on an adventure today.

I'm tired yet big bear I didn't sleep good last night, I had a bad nightmare and dreamt I was drowning.

I had another dream I was falling off of a cliff. I quickly woke up, but you were still sleeping. I was able to calm myself down and go back to sleep. I was glad that the dream was over.

"Why didn't you play the flute this morning?"

"I didn't feel like it."

"Would you like me to play the flute now?"

"No,"

I want to get things ready for our adventure. Big bear then let's get my things together and go. Lena had a small satchel that she would where.

She kept me food in it and a piece of flint, she al kept her necklace in the satchel too. She would always carry the satchel around with her.

He took off his head dress and set it down on the ground next to the blanket in the tee pee. Big bear walked out of the tee pee and took a good look around.

There were me songbirds singing. Big Bear loved to hear the songbirds sing, they would make him feel all relaxed.

There were two songbirds, the one songbird was yellow. The other one was all brown, the yellow songbird perched itself on the top of the tee pee. There was a cool breeze blowing, it felt good to Big Bear.

There was a row of pine trees that were off to the right of the tee pee. The tee pee was in the shade, off to the left side of the tee pee, was another two tee pees.

These tee pees were the same size as Big Bears tee pee. Like a hundred yards away was the small creek, fifty feet away to the left of the tee pee were large boulders.

Big Bear would often meet up with the other two tribes early each morning. He liked to wake up early, he would be awake before Lena.

Lena was a heavy sleeper, and it would take a lot to wake her up. One-time he accidentally bumped into Lena while she was sleeping, and she just rolled over and kept on sleeping.

He was glad that she didn't awake. But today Big Bear wanted to journey up to the ridge that he calls the sacred spot.

At this spot he always feels calm and relaxed, it takes a day or for him to reach the sacred spot.

He climbs up a few steep hills to get to the scared spot. Last year it took him two days just to reach the ridge, he had gotten lost two times but eventually was able to find his way.

Last year he didn't have Lena with him, but instead she stayed with the neighboring tribe for a while. Big bear doesn't like to leave Lena's side.

Chapter 6: On Their Way

He doesn't like to take her with him on his journeys, he doesn't want her to get hurt. But today he was going to take her with. Lena came out of the tee pee; she had a smile on her face.

"How are you feeling this morning?"

"I feel good and I'm ready for the journey today."

"I have my satchel ready and do I."

"How are you doing today big bear?"

"I feel good."

"I'm ready to go"

"Let's go then"

Lena said make sure that you have all the supplies that you want to take with.

I have everything I want to take along; Let's get going. Big bear always kept a compass in his satchel.

He happened to look at his compass and they were headed in the direction of

North, the sun felt good. It was seventy-five degrees outside.

Lena always wore her hair back in a ponytail. Sometimes she would have her hair pulled back and would have pigtails. Big bear was beginning to think about food.

Along the way he would stop at a blue berry patch and pick me blue berries and eat them. The blue berry bushes were an hours walk from where big bears tee pee was.

Big bear was still a half an hour or away from where the blue berry bushes were. Lena didn't like to eat blue berries; she says that they taste too sweet and give her a stomachache.

Big bear picked a hand full of blueberries, He just can't get enough of them. One-time he got a bad stomachache from eating too many blueberries.

He ate two handfuls of blue berries. Big Bears stomach was grumbling, and he couldn't make it stop.

Lena heard his stomach grumbling and asked what's wrong with your stomach? It's just complaining because I didn't eat much this morning.

Big Bear it's not good to not eat, once we get to the blue berry bushes I want you to pick me blueberries and eat them.

"How about if we go hunting later for a deer"

"I'm feeling hungry big bear."

Yes, we can go hunting for a deer later this afternoon. I'll hunt the deer for you big bear if you want.

I brought my long bow and a few arrows. You know Big Bear I like to hunt with my long bow.

They were walking across a field of tall yellow grass. The grass came up to their knees.

Lena knew that there could be a rattle snake hiding somewhere in the grass. Big Bear kept on watching and did Lena. Lena found a stick laying on the ground and leaned over and picked it up.

She carried it the whole time they were walking through the tall yellow grass.

Within a few minutes they were all the way through the grass.

They came upon a valley, there was green grass and a lot of green bushes that were surrounding the valley.

They carefully walked through the bushes and were careful to not walk into the sticker bushes that were inside the green bushes.

The sticker bushes had big thorns on them, Lena and Big Bears cloths were made out of prong horn hide.

The hide would give them good protection against sticker bushes and the cold. Lena and big bear make all of their own cloths.

Lena likes to make cloths for the other tribe's kids, Lena loves to help out wherever she can. The ground was becoming more uneven, there were a lot of small rocks in their way.

They carefully stepped over the rocks. Lena stepped on a rock, and it almost caused her to over tread her ankle. She let out a groan and said ouch.

Big Bear heard her say ouch and asked her what's a matter? She replied I just accidentally stepped on a rock and almost hurt my ankle.

I'm okay, let's continue and hopefully we can get to the ridge early. He looked up and saw a red-tailed hawk flying just above them.

He kept on circling around looking for something to eat, it let out a screech and flew out of sight. He used to have a red-tailed hawk as a pet.

He had caught it when it was just a few months old and raised it into adult hood. He would catch mice for it, Big Bear would let the red-tailed hawk perch itself on his right shoulder.

He has this red-tailed hawk for like five years and then one day the hawk died of old age. Lena didn't like the hawk though.

She thought that it was dangerous for him to have a bird as a pet. But she was happy after the bird had passed away.

Big Bear buried the bird near his ding, the sun was now all the way up in the sky. The sun was hot and felt good.

The sweat began to run down his face and Lena's face. They didn't have anything with them to wipe the sweat off of their foreheads. Big Bear and Lena stopped by the local creek and swam around in the creek to cool off.

The creeks water was cold, but it was hot outside. Big Bear didn't walk all the way into the creek, he just walked until he was knee deep in the creek. But Lena had walked all the way into the creek and was swimming around.

The creek wasn't too deep, it was just like four and half feet deep. Lena was five foot eight tall.

Although Big bear was a little bit taller, then her though. Lena had took off her satchel and laid it down on the bank of the creek.

Big Bear bent down and grabbed her satchel and held onto it, until she got out of the creek. She had a few blueberries lying in her satchel, she had a small piece of flint in her satchel.

The compass wasn't too big, it was just small enough to fit inside the satchel. He had a piece of flint in his satchel.

For an emergency he kept the flint in his satchel. He was good at starting fires without flint, but using flint is easier to start a fire with. He was going to make a fire today to help Lena and him to dry out their cloths.

It was now midday and Lena, and Big Bear were going to get to the ridge earlier than they figured they would. Lena slowly and carefully walked out of the creek; she began to shiver a little bit.

"Are you cold?"

"Yes"

Chapter 7: Working Together

I didn't think the water was going to be cold. It's just the beginning of the springtime, the creek unfroze a few weeks ago.

"Would you like me to start a fire for you?"

"Yes"

Let me go and gather me wood I'll be right back.

"Can I help you gather me tinder Big Bear?"

"Sure, you can."

They walked around the woods and found a row of trees. Big Bear broke off me branches and carried them to an area of flat ground.

He placed the wood down on the ground and kneeled down and waited for Lena to bring the tinder.

He reached in his satchel and brought out a piece of flint and relaxed there until Lena came over with the tinder to start a fire. A few minutes went by, and Lena still was not anywhere near where Big Bear was.

Big Bear was getting concerned that something happened to her he stood back up and began to wander around where he thought she might be.

He heard me branches breaking and was not sure what was making the noise. It sounded like a bear, or something was walking around the woods.

Big Bear walked further into the woods and looked off to his left and saw Lena. She was beneath a big pine tree that had large branches. She was trying to look on the ground for something.

He walked over to her and asked where have you been? I've been worried about you. I’m doing good, I was just looking around for tinder. I found me and I was just going to head back.

How about we both look in the same place for wood. I don't want to see you get lost on me, I won't get lost.

I like to worry a lot; I love you too much to just forget about you. I love you too big bear. Lena gave him a hug.

Thank you for being loving, the fire that big bear started was small but kept him and Lena warm. Lena took off her clothes and laid down next to the fire.

She handed her cloths to him; he placed her cloths next to the fire. It shouldn't take long for your cloths to dry.

I'm feeling warm, I don't want you to be naked too long. All of a sudden Big Bear heard a howling noise somewhere off in the distance.

"What was that?"

"It was just a coyote howling off in the distance."

It's nothing to be worried about. Now how about if you check your cloths and see if they're dry. Lena bent over and checked her cloths.

Her pants and top felt a little cold, but they were dry. Lena looked at him and said how about if we continue on and put out the fire, we're going to continue on. I need to sit down for a while, my legs are getting tired.

"Would you like me to rub them?"

"No"

"How long do you want to spend at the ridge Big Bear?"

"I would like to spend a day or two up at the ridge."

"What would you like to do up at the ridge?"

"I would like to do me meditation."

"How about you?"

"I'll meditate too."

I've not meditated for a while; I like to meditate at least twice a day.

"How about you big bear?"

"I meditate just once a day."

"Sometimes after I meditate I feel tired."

"Do you always feel tired after meditation?"

"No"

Just sometimes, I enjoy going deep into meditation. I've been having a lot of dreams lately.

"What have they been about?"

"About all kinds of different things, one time I dreamt that I was an eagle soaring through the sky."

Then another dream that I had was that I was a grizzly bear being hunted by a hunter.

"Did you wake up nervous?"

"No"

I woke up just like I do every morning. My favorite dream was the dream when I was an eagle soaring above a valley. The valley was green and there were bushes all over the sides of the valley.

"Did you hunt and kill anything while you were the eagle in the dream?"

"I don't remember if I did or not."

"Did have a dream that you were an animal?"

"No," I can't say I ever have.

"Hopefully one day you'll have a dream like that."

"Are you scared of having dreams?"

"No, I'm not."

It's just at the end of the day I'm tired that I fall asleep, I don't have enough time to be able to go into the dream world.

Very rarely do I fall into the dream world. Sometimes my soul leaves my body for a short period of time.

"How does that make you feel big bear?"

"It feels good but can sometimes make me feel tired."

"What's the longest period of time your soul has left your body?"

"It's left for more than an hour"

"How do you know that if there's no way you can tell time?"

"That's a good question."

I'm ready to get going again, let me put out the fire and we'll go. Big bear put out the fire, smoke came out of the fire, and it went out. Big Bear and Lena began to start walking on through me thick vegetation.

There were me sticker bushes, they had large thorns on them. Lena and big bear were careful not to walk into the thorns.

I enjoy these long walks with you. Two red tailed Hawks flew overhead, they let out a screeching sound. The one red tailed hawk was missing a few feathers from its left wing.

It seemed like it had got into a fight with another hawk or me other kind of creature. Up ahead of them were a large flowing river, there were a lot of sharp slippery rocks in the middle of the river.

The water had a fast-moving current. At the bottom of the river were white water Rapids, they were used to seeing rivers like this one.

They would find the easiest and safest place to cross the river. He looked at the river and saw that there was a large beaver dam in the middle of it.

Lena said look at the mother and its baby, beavers are cute.

"Do you agree with me?"

"Yes, I do"

I've seen many beavers in my time and I hunt them for their pelts. They are worth a few dollars; I sell them to the civilized man or other tribes. You have told me all about that before, it's nothing new to me.

"Could you teach me how you prepare the skins for tanning?"

"Yes," I can, and I will.

"Would you mind if we hunted the Beavers?"

"No," I don't at all.

"Can I borrow your long bow?"

"Sure, you can"

Lena gently handed her long bow to Big Bear and al handed him an arrow. There was a sharp arrowhead at the end of the arrow.

Chapter 8: The Trek

There were turkey feathers used as the feathers for on the arrow. To shoot a long bow, it's all instinct. There are no sights, let me sneak up closer on the beavers. I'm not going to shoot the mother beaver and her baby.

I saw another beaver swimming along; it was much larger than the three beavers that you see there. Big Bear took his time and got ready for a good shot.

He slowly pulled back the string and let the arrow fly into the air. The arrow flew straight across the river and struck the large beaver right behind its left shoulder.

It tried to walk a little but fell over onto its left side, it remained laying on the bank. But it was on the other side of the river.

He knew that he was going to have to figure out a good way to get across the river. Lena asked how about if I go scout out the river and I'll be right back, Lena walked at a fast pace.

She kept on walking along the river, she kept on looking left to right for a good way to cross the river.

She looked ahead and saw that there was a shallow part of the river, there was a tree that had fallen across the river.

She figured that her and big bear could easily cross the river, the tree looked like it was all moldy and was beginning to fall apart.

All the bark had fallen off of the fallen tree, it was a big tree, and had moss all over it. She knew that moss was very slippery when wet, the fallen tree was halfway submerged in water.

Lena bent down and felt the tree, me pieces of the tree fell into the river below it. There were a few branches that were barely hanging onto the tree. Lena put me pressure on one of the branches and it fell off and went into the river below.

The water in the river below was flowing fast and was loud. Lena could barely hear herself think the river was loud, suddenly the wind began to blow. The one feather in her hair flew out and flew into the river below, it was just a turkey feather.

She wasn't worried about losing the feather. The afternoon sun was hot, and Lena began to sweat.

She still wasn't sure that it was safe or not to walk across the river over the fallen tree. The wind was blowing at five miles per hour.

Suddenly an eagle flew over, it was looking for something. It was flying pretty high in the sky; it was the same height in the sky as the clouds were.

It had its talons down and looked like it was ready to catch something. It had its head down really searching for prey.

They were walking up a steep hill, the hill was all muddy. It was hard to climb up, sheer determination they both were able to climb up the hill and get to the top. There was a slight wind blowing from the south.

The sky was growing darker as time went on, there were a few clouds floating through the sky. There two gray clouds in the sky.

For these were rain clouds. Big bear said to Lena it seems like it is going to rain. Don't worry about it I like to walk in the rain.

I prefer not to though, don't say that. It's sometimes good to get stuck walking in the rain. Off to their left a crow flew in and landed almost next to them and Big Bear. He said this crow is a sign of bad travels.

"What do you mean?"

"When I was just a boy the tribe elder taught me about what certain animals mean when you see them. The crow means bad travels and that you'll have to stop traveling and wait until the crow flies away."

Then you can continue on, why don't we just continue on walking anyway. No, it's not a good idea.

I don't want anything negative to happen to neither one of us. Then we'll continue standing here until the crow flies away.

The crow was looking for something it kept on walking around Big Bear and Lena. It kept its eyes on Big Bear and Lena, its eyes were black and looked evil.

This crow is making me nervous; I have a feeling something is going to happen to us.

No, I don't think, don't let the crow look into your eyes and scare you. It'll be alright I promise Lena.

Big Bear looked down at the crow and kept on watching the crows every movement. The crow began to peck the ground.

Then it brought it beak back up out of the ground and there was a worm hanging out of its mouth. It quickly swallowed the worm and looked back at big bear.

Big Bear didn't care the crow was looking at him. The crow began to flap its wings but didn't want to fly away.

Lena said you know I don't think this crow wants to leave anytime on. Don't worry Lena the crow probably will fly away on, or I'll make him fly away.

I think this crow needs to go. Big Bear kicked me dirt up at the crow, the crow flew away into the distance. It was a sigh of relief to big bear and Lena, now we can go on with our journey.

"Are you still feeling good?"

"Yes."

Up ahead of them was a few tall pine trees, it was like a forest full of pine trees. The pine trees offered a lot of shade and it felt good to the both of them, I love walking through the woods like this.

"How about you?"

"I love going anywhere with you."

I love you too, hopefully we can be by the ridge before sundown. That's wishful thinking, but I don't think so. We walk at a good pace, but it still take us all of the night to get to the ridge. I'm not going to walk all night, I'd rather just rest.

"Do you know where Keeko is?"

"No," I don't I'm very upset that he's missing.

He's my brother and I loved him very much, he has a gentle soul. Every minute with him was wonderful and now he's gone and not in my life. It's those space people that took him away, I'm mad at them.

I wish I could find out where they took him too, I didn't know that Keeko was taken by the space people. I thought he just wondered out of camp and got lost.

No, they took him the space people. I'm sorry to hear that big bear, I hope we can find him.

We will in good time, we haven't been to a sweat lodge in a while. It's been almost a year since we have been to a sweat lodge.

"Why don't we go to the nearby sweat lodge and spend time with another tribe of people?"

"I know where the local sweat lodge is around this area."

We'll go to the sweat lodge after we spend a day on the ridge, and I can spend half of the day meditating.

"How long would you like to stay at the sweat lodge?"

"I would like to stay there for at least half of the day."

"Didn't you tell me a story that one time you passed out in a sweat lodge?"

"Yes."

I was sitting in the sweat lodge and the temperature kept on increasing, on it was unbearable to me, and I had trouble breathing and each breath I took made my lungs burn.

I was trying to stand up and I fell down and fainted. There were two other Native American warriors in the sweat lodge with me.

The one native warrior had to quickly get me out of the sweat lodge. My body was soaked head to toe in sweat, the one warrior poured cold water on my face to wake me up.

When I awoke I asked them what had happened to me, and they said my body wasn't used to the hot temperatures.

They said that I had bad energy stuck inside of me. They told me that I would have to regain my strength and rest for half of the day, then I could come back and try the sweat lodge again later in the evening.

I'm strong willed; I rested and went back to the sweat lodge. This time my body was able to handle the intense heat. The two warriors looked at me and said you are one tough women. They said that usually women don't go to sweat lodges, just the Warriors do.

"What did you say to that?"

"I just said OKAY."

"How many sweat lodges have you been to Big Bear?"

"I've been to eight of them in the last few years."

I was able to handle the heat, the other Native American warriors in the sweat lodges I have been to have passed out.

"How comes you don't pass out?"

"I'm just tough, I'm used to the hot heat."

Honestly I don't think women should go into sweat lodges.

"Why not?"

"Like you were saying earlier that it got too hot."

I don't think women can handle the hot steam. It's just makes them weaker I believe; I didn't get weaker from the sweat lodge. Today is such a nice day. The sky is blue and there's a gentle breeze going, it's a great day for a walk.

It always feels good to have good weather, I've been through me bad hailstorms before Big Bear.

I have been through me hailstorms too, the hail hurt when it would bounce off of my head. The hailstorm lasted for a few hours, and I was glad when it was over.

"Where were you headed when the hailstorm began?"

"I was taking a short walk over to the neighboring tribe."

It would take me an hour to get to the other tribe, this tribe is called the cassias. The cassias are a rather large tribe.

They are made of twenty-three members; they have many trained warriors. There warriors have won many battles with other tribes.

Chapter 9: Obstacles

This particular tribe was always trying to improve their weapons, they have a few different weapons that they use in battle.

They use the long bow and muzzleloaders and spears, I thought they only used spears for hunting. No, they use them in battle.

I learn a lot from being around you, I learn from you too. All of a sudden the wind began to pick up and made it colder outside.

Which direction are we headed in, we are heading towards the North. All of a sudden a black cloud came over head and it began to rain.

It looks like we are going to get stuck in the rain, oh that's alright I don't mind a little rain, me neither.

I think the rain is refreshing and cools me down. The rain continued on and on was coming down heavier.

I think we need to find shelter; it's going to be a down pour outside and it's not good to be walking around in a bad rainstorm and being in wet clothing.

If you look over to your right there's a small cave and I think, we should spend the rest of the day in the cave. Then I'll go and gather me wood to make a fire.

I'm going to gather as much wood as I can Lena. Alright then I'll be waiting for you in the cave, the rain kept on coming down.

Big Bear looked off to his left and saw a few pine trees. They had a lot of branches on them, he broke off me of the branches and carried the branches with him.

He had to walk one hundred feet over to where the cave was. You gathered the wood up quickly.

"How did you gather the wood quickly?"

"I just ran over to a few pine trees and broke the branches off of them and here I am."

"Did you gather any moss?"

"No," I didn't, alright then give me a moment and I'll go gather me moss.

"Where are you going to find moss if we are not close to a river or creek?"

"I know where to find peat moss. I have learned to look for moss in old logs and on old rotting trees."

I hope you can find me, I will don't worry. Lena quickly walked over towards a thicket.

There was an old tree stump and a freshly Fallon oak tree, the oak tree had a lot of branches coming out of it. Lena bent down and took a closer look at the branches.

She broke off a few branches and carried them with her, she continued on and came across a tree stump. The tree stump was rotting away, and all the bark had fallen off of it.

There was me moss growing all around the left side of the tree stump. Lena bent down on one knee and was careful not to waste any of the moss. She careful picked the moss off of the tree stump.

She placed the moss in her satchel, she made sure that there was more than enough moss. The moss was a bright green color and had a texture of that of mud.

Lena didn't mind getting her hands dirty, she was used to getting mud on her hands. It didn't take Lena long to get back to the cave.

I'm glad it didn't take you too long to get back here Lena. No, I don't like to waste any time doing what I need. Her long hair was all wet and her cloths were dripping with water.

Lena we better get you dried off and your cloths dried off too, Big Bear bent down and began to rub two sticks together.

He rubbed them together for a while and all of a sudden a fire started. The tinder caught fire and Big Bear blew on the small flame.

The flame grew larger and big bear placed the moss on the ground in front of them. The branches caught fire; it was now a good size fire. Big Bear and Lena had stand back from the fire.

The flame was flickering back and forth from the wind blowing in, it was a strong wind. I'm getting nervous about the way the wind is blowing.

"Why's that?"

When the wind blows this way it usually brings in a bad thunder and lightning storm. The wind is blowing from the west, I've predicted storms correctly every time before.

I suggest that we go and get me more branches from the trees and make like a small shelter to protect us from the high winds. If the rain blows in from the West, I think there are enough branches to make a half decent shelter.

Lena was having difficulty keeping the sticks together for the shelter. The sticks kept on falling down and kept on exposing them to the high wind and rain.

The cave kept them dry, but the high winds were brutal. Big Bears cheeks were rosy, red, he was getting cold. The wind wouldn't stop blowing hard.

Hold on Lena let me help you finish putting up the temporary shelter. I'm good at building sweat lodges and shelters. Big Bear took the five sticks and began to push the sticks into the ground.

The sticks were sticking straight up out of the ground, he took a small thicker stick and placed it right underneath the thin sticks.

He had to keep rubbing his hands together to keep his hands warm.

"What's wrong?"

"My hands are cold; I was just trying to warm my hands up."

"How do you feel?"

I'm getting cold, you'll have to get closer to the fire. The wind almost blew out the fire.

The flame flickered again and this time the flame got too close to Lena's leg and almost burned it. Lena quickly jumped up and backed away from the fire.

Big Bear saw Lena jump up and it disrupted him. He had a bewildered look on his face.

"Are you alright?"

"No," I almost got my leg burned.

"Does your leg hurt?"

"No," luckily my leg is alright.

My pants almost got burned, I'm glad you are okay. Why don't you sit down, I'll sit down once the work is done. sometimes when I sit too long, my legs tend to cramp up. Big bear looked down and noticed that one of the sticks in the ground was beginning to fall over. They had fallen fast asleep.

The cold wind kept on blowing, but it stopped raining. The fires flame kept on flicking from all the wind, the temporary shelter held up just fine.

Big Bear happened to look up and saw that the sun was beginning to rise, big bear heard me birds chirping nearby. He rolled over to his other side and fell back asleep.

He slept good but still he was tired he looked at Lena, she was still fast asleep. Big bear felt her right hand and it felt as cold as ice. Then he took his hand and held her right hand until it warmed up.

During the whole time Lena didn't even wake up, big bear ran his fingers through her long black hair. She still didn't move a muscle.

Big Bear was glad that she was sleeping soundly, because she usually doesn't sleep that good. She rolled over to her left side; she saw that Big Bear was running his fingers through her hair.

"What are you doing?"

"I'm just running my fingers through your hair."

"Are you going to get up?"

"I'm going to get up"

I think we should both get up now and begin hunting for deer.

"What do you think?"

"I think we should continue to rest and in the early afternoon go hunting for a deer. I don't think we should be wasting time."

Let's just get on with the plan. Besides that, I'm cold.

"How can you be cold if you're sitting right by the fire?"

"I don't know"

"Would you like to wear my shirt?"

"No," I'll be alright.

Big Bear saw a hawk flying around outside of the cave. The hawk looked like it was looking for something, it kept on circling around. It made one final swoop; it landed a few feet from the outside of the cave.

It began to dig down into the ground, he looked and there was a little field mouse running around in circles.

The hawk caught the mouse within a minute, the mouse didn't have time to escape.

He had brought along the flute; the flute was in his back pocket. He was careful not to break the flute by leaning on it. Lena quickly stood up and took a look around.

"Why did you stand up fast?"

"I heard a squeaking and it really annoyed me, I stood up and wanted to investigate what was happening"

The noise that you heard was a red-tailed hawk catching a field mouse, I didn't think that the little noise would wake you up, it did.

"Are you going back to sleep?"

"No," I want to get up and get on with our adventure.

"How about if you would wait here and I would just go hunting for a deer?"

“No,” I would rather the both of us go hunting.

I don't want anything to happen to you Lena, nothing would happen to me. I know how to use a bow and how to protect myself, I’m here to protect you.

“Why don't you get up and let's go hunting right now?”

“I’m ready to go.”

Big Bear slowly got up; he was feeling kind of shaky. His left knee was aching.

“What's wrong?”

“My left knee is just aching.”

“Why’s that?”

“I have a cramp.”

"Do you want me to rub your knee for you?"

"No," I should be just fine.

"Once I'm up and moving it'll feel better."

"Are you going to put out the fire or should I?"

"I'll stump out the fire"

Big Bear carefully took his right foot and stumped out the fire, smoke came up from the fire.

Now the fire was out, him and Lena began walking towards the East, the sun was now halfway up in the sky.

The heat from the sun felt good, I hope you're ready for another long day of walking. I’m always ready for a long walk Lena.

“Are you getting to feeling any warmer?”

“Yes,” I’m warming up.

Chapter 10: Exploration

My hands are no longer cold, I was getting worried about you. No, I'm warming up just fine. He could hear a crow squeaking in the distance, it was blue skies and there were no clouds in the sky.

It was quiet outside, except for the crow. Big Bear took his left hand and held onto Lena's left hand, they walked for a while through the valley.

There was grass growing all around and there were a few thick green bushes growing. me of the bushes were tall, which would make it difficult to get around them.

Some of the small trees were swaying in the wind, the wind was still howling and didn't let up. We should be arriving at the ridge on, he have been walking a far way.

"What's the first thing that you want to do once we are at the ridge?"

"I would sit down and get relaxed and do some meditation. I would remain in a meditative state for a good while or until I would wake up."

I think I need to meditate more often; I agree with that, I hardly ever see you meditate with the others in the tribe. It just takes me a while to settle down somedays.

"What do you settle down?"

"I mean when I feel relaxed."

Lena and Big Bear kept on walking until they were almost at the bottom of the ridge. They were going to have to climb up and over a few boulders to reach the ridge.

"Are you ready to climb over the boulders?"

"Yes," I am.

I'm excited to get to the top of the ridge, I enjoy climbing Lena. Lena was almost half up the boulders and her left leg slipped.

Hold on Lena Let me help you, I would have never made it up without you.

It didn't take you long at all to climb over the boulders, no when I was a young child I liked to climb.

That was difficult for me to climb up, you look like you need to sit down for a while Lena. I think I need to sit for a while Big Bear, I'll sit right next to you until you feel better.

We're almost at the top of the ridge. All this climbing tires me out big Bear, I just have to catch my breath and we can go on climbing up the ridge. Sometime later Lena stood and began walking further up the ridge with big Bear.

We're going to have to climb up one more steep hill, I should be able to climb up the last steep hill.

"Are you sure you are going to be alright?"

"Yes," I will be.

I just get tired sometimes and have to rest.

"Is your knee still feeling good Big Bear?"

"Yes."

Lena took her time and slowly climbed up the steep hill, this time she was able to climb right up with no problems. She didn't slip at all.

Big Bear lost grip in his left hand and almost fell backwards, he was able to get his grip again and reached the top of the hill.

"Are you alright back there?"

"Yes," I'm taking my time to get to the top of the hill.

I don't know how I was able to get to the top of the hill before you, I had slipped climbing up the hill. I was able to get up the hill, your hands are all muddy because I was on my hands and knees climbing.

There's more mud on your hands then on your feet, I don't mind a little mud on me, I'll clean my hands with the grass. Lena and Big Bear reached the top of the ridge.

There was a gently breeze blowing. He looked up in the air and saw an owl flying along through the woods.

It landed on a branch of a tall pine tree, it looked like it was hunting for something to eat. It had big yellow eyes; it had its head turned all the way towards the left.

Its talons were very long and razor sharp, the owls feathers were a grayish color. It had its left wing stretched out; it was picking at its feathers with its sharp beak.

It kept on picking through his feathers for a long while, then stopped. It had white feathers on its chest, it was missing a feather or two from its tail.

It made a hooting sound, then flew away again and went further into the thick green vegetation.

It was now the beginning of spring, the weather was nice, and it was warm outside.

Big Bear bent down and wiped the mud off of his hands in the grass, he happened to look down at the valley.

He saw a silver spaceship fly over the valley, it hovered just for a minute. Then flew away, Lena didn't see the spaceship. Big Bear couldn't believe what he had just saw.

"Lena looked over at him and asked what's wrong?"

"I just saw a spaceship."

"Where?"

"It was hovering above the valley below."

I'm surprised that I didn't see it, it probably would have scared you. No, I'm not afraid of anything, I don't understand why you always see the strange things and I never do.

"Do you think that the space people are going to try to take us away?"

"No," I don't think

Now let's go on and not worry about what the space people are doing.

"Do you mind if I hold onto your left-hand?"

"No," I wouldn't mind. I like to hold your hand Big Bear; it makes me feel safe and secure.

He happened to look over and noticed that Lena was walking with a slight limp in her left leg.

"What's wrong with your leg?"

"It just aches."

Last night I got a bad cramp in my leg, and it still aches today. The more I walk the better it's going to get; Lena's long black hair was blowing in the wind. Big Bear kept his eyes up at the sky.

He kept on watching the sky, the sky was blue and looked like it did any other day. There was nothing unusual, a few more steps and we are where I want to be.

It felt like we were never going to get here, don't start complaining now. We are now here, there was a brown tree trunk right ahead of Big Bear.

The bark was falling off of the tree trunk, the ground was kind of ft and there was a lot of mud. Big Bear sat down on the tree trunk, he stretched out his long legs and uncrossed his muscular arms.

When Big Bear was a teenager he liked to Indian leg wrestle with the other kids from the nearby tribe, he would win most of the time.

But lost once or twice to a kid that was bigger and had more muscle mass then what he had. He beat Big Bear twice in one day.

But Big Bear never gave up, he tried a third time and mustered up all the remaining strength that he had a was able to win.

His opponent couldn't believe that he won. He just figured that Big Bear was just going to let him win, but he was wrong.

Lena let go of his left hand and walked over to a green bush. There me sticker bushes wrapped around the bush.

The sticker bushes had short stubby thorns on them, Lena was careful not to walk into the thorns.

She was looking at the bush because a beautiful butterfly landed on the bush. It was all yellow; it's wings were flapping a mile a minute.

Its body was a brownish color, it stayed on the bush for a while and didn't flap its wings. It seemed like it was comfortable there.

Then another butterfly flew over to the bush and landed right next to the other butterfly.

All of a sudden a cool breeze came through and flew away both of the butterfly's. The butterflies flew into the sky.

They kept on flapping their wings and gliding along through the open sky. Lena looked over at the tree she was standing next to, and a gray squirrel was running up and down the branches at the top of the tree.

The tree had many branches; It was missing me branches on the side that Lena was leaning on. There was a large knot in the tree.

This tree must of have had large roots. A thick brown root was sticking out of the ground near where Lena was standing. Lena was thinking about sitting down on the trees root but decided not to.

She liked to stand for a while. There was thick green grass growing all around the tree trunk that big bear was sitting on. The grass that was growing near the large tree was an unhealthy yellow color, the blades of the yellow grass were four foot tall. Lena finally decided to sit down on the root, she leaned back into the tree and stretched out there.

She thought to herself this is a good time for me to meditate, she leaned her head back and closed her eyes. Big Bear still didn't close his eyes, he was on the lookout for the space people. The wind began to pick up again. It felt good to him because he was hot, sweat poured down his forehead.

He reached up with his left hand and itched his left ear. After a few minutes he stopped scratching his left ear. He just had me dry skin on his left ear. Big Bear looked over at Lena.

Chapter 11: Nature

He was glad to see that she was relaxing and that she was comfortable. However big bear was not very comfortable and looked around for another place to sit.

The ground was too muddy to sit down on, the grass was kind of wet from the dew of last night. The sun was bright today, every time he would look up at the sky the bright sun would bother his sensitive eyes.

His hair get very long, as he aged the color of his hair changed from a dark brown color to the color gray.

Big Bear didn't mind that his hair was turning gray, he was glad to have such long hair. Big bears hair wasn't as long as Lena's hair, it was close. His hair was put into two ponytails, this is the way he preferred to have his hair. Big Bear wasn't planning on having a haircut anytime on, he looked down at his moccasins and saw that they had mud all over them.

The mud was caked onto the bottom of the moccasins, he leaned over and picked up a small stick. He took the stick and tried to get off me of the mud off of them.

He tried again and again and eventually got me of the caked mud off, there was a lot of dried mud on the sides of his moccasins.

The laces were beginning to become untied again he bent down and retied the laces.

The laces were a light brown color, he tied a good tight not. Lena was still laid back against the tree slowly falling into a meditative state.

Big Bear stood up and looked to his left then right. He saw a large Boulder behind him.

It didn't want to sit on such a hard surface, he was looking for a nice place to sit that wasn't muddy. He walked through the tall yellow grass.

The grass was not too tall, but Big Bear looked down and saw that something was slithering through the grass. It was a rattle snake, it rattled its tail and warned Big Bear.

He watched as the snake was slithering along, the snake didn't see him right away, but Big Bear saw him first. He bent down and grabbed the snake by the back of its neck and held it nice and tight.

The snake was trying to get out of the grasps of his strong hands, the snake became limp in his hands. But it still was moving.

He kept on holding onto the snake, he laid it down on the tree trunk. He wasn't feeling hungry for snake, he figured that he would just let the dead snake lay there.

He didn't want to bother Lena, he walked further away from where she was sitting. She was sitting Indian style with her legs crossed, she kept her arms all the way stretched out.

While he had stayed rested against the tree. Big Bear looked at a tall oak tree that fifty feet away from him, he saw bees flying around the tops branches of the tree.

He looked closer and saw a large bees nest up in the tree. He quickly got as far away from the tree as possible, no bees flew near him. Big Bear had learned his lesson about bees.

When he was a young boy he was fearless, and he liked to eat honey. He would always rob the bees of their precious honey and they would sting him as many times as they could.

He was riddled with bee stings all over his face and chest and arms, he had me many red spots on his body. That it looked like he had a bad sun burn.

A bee even stung him on the tip of his nose, but it didn't hurt as bad as the bee sting that was near his left eye. A bee stung him almost on his eye lid.

Once he was done getting all the honey from the hive he would roll his body in me fresh mud. This would help the stings to stop stinging and would cool them.

Big Bear was much older and intelligent, lately he would rather avoid the bees then fight with them and get all stung up. Pain always makes him remember things better.

The long feathers in his hair were being blown all around, one of the feathers went flying into the air. It flew a good ten feet towards the tree with the bee's nest in it, he just ignored it.

He had plenty of other feathers, one missing didn't matter much to him. There was short skinny tree off to his left, there were a bunch of dandelions growing around the base of the tree, the tree wasn't in good shape.

The center of the tree was all black and slowly rotting away. Many of its branches were gone, they must have fallen off.

At the very top of the tree, it was all black. It looked like it had been struck by lightning a beautiful little yellow bird landed on the lower branch of the tree. It perched itself perfectly on the branch.

It began to chirp; it bend down and began to peck the branch that it was perched on. Big Bear kept on observing the little bird.

He looked closer at the branch and noticed that there were black ants crawling all over the branch of the tree. The little bird had a quick meal off of the ants.

There were many ants crawling along the branch. The ants disturbed the bird, and it flew away deeper into the woods. He was in an area that was open with not much foliage around him.

A gray squirrel scurried along by Lena, it almost crawled over Lena. It seemed to have no fear of humans, it crawled closer to Lena. It quickly ran over Lena's chest and continued up into the tree.

Lena didn't even move a muscle when the squirrel ran over her chest. She was in such a deep trance. Big Bear brought out his binoculars, he looked down at the valley. He saw a black bear, that was standing up on his hind legs. It was sniffing the air and had a scar near its left eye.

After a short while the bear went back down on its legs, there was a tall brown bush next to the where the bear was standing.

There were me sticker bushes lying on top of the brown bush, the thorns were very sharp.

The bear seemed like it didn't have good eyesight, it accidentally walked into the brown bush. A thorn stuck to its muzzle, it let out a groan and backed away from the bush.

Big Bear was sitting close to Lena. Lena was snoring. She had her arms crossed. Big Bear looked down at the valley again, the bear had not moved far from where it originally was.

It rolled over onto its back and was acting very playful. It looked like it was using the ground to scratch its back, it had long claws coming out of its large paws.

The one long claw looked like it was bent back and ready to fall off, the bear continued to roll around. Big Bear was getting tired of watching the bear just roll around.

The bears black fur was turning brown. There was a lot of fresh brown mud all over the bears back and side.

After a while the bear stood back and began to slowly walk along the edge of the valley. The bear opened its mouth and let out a great yawn, he could see all of his sharp canines.

Big Bear thought it must of took of a lot of pressure for the tooth to be broken, the bear had me bald spots on its left side. Big Bear could tell that the bear was an old Sal.

The bear kept on walking slowly, it looked up towards the ridge. It sniffed one more time then it slowly retreated back into the deep brush, he was glad to see the bear.

There was a small patch of ground that was not muddy. There were me dandelions growing on the small patch of ground.

There was a wild mushroom growing. It was all brown and had a few spots of white on it. Big Bear realized that this mushroom wasn't the kind that you can eat but is used for medicinal purposes. Big

Bear likes to eat mushrooms every now and then.

He was sitting up, but his back began to bother him. It was aching, and he took his right hand and began to rub the middle of his back.

He got me relief and decided to lay down and get more comfortable, he was about to lay down and a small rock was thrown at him from behind.

He looked behind him and didn't anything, this really irritated him. He walked further into the woods; he still didn't see anything. He looked and saw a few tall pine trees.

The pine trees had long branches and there were many pinecones beneath the pine tree. He reached down and picked up one of the pinecones.

There was no sign of anyone or anything around, he couldn't think of what could have thrown the rock. He thought maybe a spirit could have done it, he quickly forgot about that idea.

He began to think it was the space people playing games with him, he began to increasingly get angered. He was now deep in the woods that he looked back and could no longer see Lena.

Chapter 12: The Sighting

He just continued to walk on deeper into the woods, he almost tripped over a rock. There was a long root coming out of the one tree that he walked past, he almost tripped over the big brown root.

He decided to sit down on the root, he had a clear view of the woods from where he was sitting.

I wanted to see more of what was going on, he climbed up the tree. He grabbed onto a thick branch and pulled himself up into the tree.

Now he could see much better, he felt relaxed up in the tree. Big Bear wasn't afraid of heights.

He kept on looking around and he was getting tired of it, then another rock was thrown. The rocks were always thrown at him from behind him. He couldn't understand, what was going on.

He looked behind him and saw nothing, he thought to himself I'm going to just ignore the rock throwing.

The rocks were not too big in size but where big enough to hurt if hit by one. He thought okay, I'm going to throw a rock and see what happens.

Big Bear climbed back down out of the tree, he reached down and picked up a rock.

He threw the rock as hard as he could in the direction of where the last rock came from. Nothing happened after he threw the rock.

Then suddenly the ground underneath his feet began to shake, the ground was splitting apart. The shaking ground almost was enough to cause Big Bear to lose his balance.

He was still able to remain standing, but he sat down on the ground and sat Indian style.

He closed his eyes and leaned back, he thought to himself I hope these mysterious happenings stop on.

He felt like he was going to panic, he knew that he was going to have to stay calm through everything that was happening.

The ground shook a second time, he still couldn't understand what was happening.

He thought to himself I better get out of here before something else happens.

He back himself away from the tree and remained standing there leaning over on the tree. The ground stopped shaking and it was a great sigh of relief.

Big Bear began to walk at a faster pace through the woods, he didn't look, and tripped over a mound of dirt.

He fell onto his side but was quickly able to get up. Once he got up he continued on running out of the woods, there was a little tree that became up rooted and big bear almost walked into it, he went on and was now out of the woods. He came into an open area.

He didn't see Lena, he thought oh no what if the space people took her away. He looked around the tree she was laying and there was still no sign of her.

The tree had a big crack in it, some of the branches had fallen off of the tree. He saw that there was large green bush a few yards away from the tree.

The foliage was green and thick, then he saw Lena. She was sitting in the thick foliage, he had to look carefully just to see Lena. Big Bear asked her why are you hiding back here? I was awoke when the ground shook twice.

But what made you come back here? I saw a spacecraft fly over the open area where I was, I didn't want it to see me. That's why I came back here.

Lena had a terrified look on her face, I need a hug I'm scared. Lena was shaking in fear, once Big Bear had given her a hug she stopped shaking.

I'm still really nervous, I won't let the space people hurt you, as long as I'm with you. I'm afraid that spacecraft is going to come back and take me away. I had a dream about that the other day Big Bear. With a sad look on his face, he said everything is going to be okay.

"Do you promise?"

"Yes"

"Now I feel better."

"Do you need another hug?"

"Yes," I do.

Big Bear hugged Lena a second time and Lena said I'm tired of the bizarre occurrences, me to. I just want my brother back, those space people really have me angry, I wish they would just leave the both of us alone.

I didn't want to deal with it anymore. But we can't just stay here, I don't think it's safe.

"What do you think?"

"I think we should stay here for one night."

"For one night."

"What's the matter with you?"

"Nothing is wrong with me"

I just don't want to leave on, okay have it your way then. If something really bad happens and those space people take us away, I'm going to blame it all on you.

"Why are you talking this way?"

"I'm concerned about my safety that's all."

I don't think it's safe here, I don't want you to leave me behind. I would never leave you behind.

"You just have to agree to disagree."

"Why aren't you afraid of the space people?"

"I have no fear."

I learned to have no fear from the Warriors, I'll fight them space people until they are all gone.

That sounds all good and all, but you don't have any weapons powerful enough to stop them. But I know where to go to get more powerful weapons to fight off the space people.

"Where's that?"

"It's defiantly not anywhere near here."

It would take me a day or two to walk there. See what I mean, you're not prepared enough to fight off the space people. Were too vulnerable to attack we need to hide from them.

We aren’t going to hide from them, we will stay out here in the open and watch for them.

“I think you have finally went out of your mind.”

“Do you want those space people to take you away?”

No, I don't but I’ll take out as many space people as I can before they take me down, I don't want to lose you. You aren't going to lose me. I’m a tough man, and I’ll stop the space people.

Just stop it, I’m very upset. I’m not thinking and just saying things. You better knock it off, or I won’t protect you.

“Is that understood?”

"Yes," it's understood.

I would never tell you to be quiet, I'm not being rude to you. I should stop acting like I do.

I want you to calm down Lena and let's plan on how were going to stop the space people. We're down here on Earth and those crazy space people are up in the sky.

If they even get too close to you, I'll beat them senseless or even kill them if I have to. You're like everything to me, that you're just trying to often me up now.

Like I said you have to think and get rid of that little attitude that you have. I only have a little attitude and I'm willing to change my attitude for you.

Why don't you come out of the thick foliage and come out here in the open

"Where I am?"

"I will once I'm ready."

"When do you think you'll be ready to come out?"

"I'll come out of here when I'm ready, please don't rush me."

I'm not trying to rush you; I'll wait here all day for you. I won't leave you alone, if something would ever happen to you then I would feel terrible.

You can't even explain to me why you think there were two earthquakes.
Honestly I don't know.

I thought it was just a natural earthly occurrence, but now I realize that the space people are involved in it.

I wish those space people were kind, but I guess that they don't care what they do. big bear I think that you should kneel down and hide here next to me Big Bear. Okay I will then.

> "How long were you able to meditate for?"
>
> 'I was able to meditate for an hour."

Chapter 13: The Hunt

It was just long enough; I didn't like getting awoke by the earthquakes. Stay here kneeled down next to me.

You know that I don't like to hide, I'd rather come out and fight. I know you would, you have no chance against the space people.

Try not to be negative Lena, I'm not trying to be negative; we both have a bad attitude.

I think that the coast is now clear, let's go back out in the open and try to relax once again. Lena and big bear held hands and walked back out in the open again.

"Are you going to sit down again?"

"No," we need to start a fire. Let's go and gather me more wood.

Hold on big bear, I think we should go hunting for a deer now. I think it's more important that we eat then start a fire. Why don't you get a fire started and I'll go hunting for a deer. No, I don't want you to go hunting on your own.

"Why not?"

"Because a few hours ago I saw a big black bear, black bears don't scare me"

It doesn’t matter, the thing is they can be dangerous and can really harm you. I hear what you’re saying, I’m going to respect your decision and stay here with you instead of going out hunting by myself I just haven’t been thinking clearly.

I tend to agree with you, it's already midafternoon and you want to go hunting. We shouldn’t waste our energy chasing around deer. We should take it easy on our bodies.

“Are you feeling okay?”

“I’m feeling just fine.”

I'm not being lazy; I just don't want to go hunting for a deer tonight. I would rather us go hunting in the early morning hours.

Besides that, it's hard to keep on hunting once it gets dark outside.

If you would get a fire started then you could see in the dark. Alright you talked me into it, let's go and see if we can get a deer.

You say that in such a boring negative voice big bear, I'm not forcing you to go out there and go hunting. I saw the bear down in the valley.

I think we should head south, alright let's go then.

"How do you know which way south is?"

"Don't you remember that I have a compass with me in my satchel."

"Yes," I do remember

You still kind of have an attitude, you know big bear I'm not trying to give you any trouble. I know but your attitude is getting really old.

"Why don't you just try to relax?"

"I was going to relax, now were hunting."

If you keep on talking loudly, you're going to scare away all the deer around here. I have been whispering so that the deer don't hear us and run away. Now I would like it if you would whisper.

We should think of a plan and not just wonder around the woods aimlessly looking for a deer.

"Are you a good tracker?"

"No," that's what I'm relying on you to do.

How about if we split up and you go to the right, and I go to the left. I think it would save us a lot of time and confusion about which way to go.

No, I disagree, let's just stay together and complete the hunt. We both need to only focus on hunting now and I'm going to stop talking that we can go. Lena and big bear walked further and further into the woods. There were a lot of big oak trees growing all around the area.

There were a few tall brown bushes sticking up from the ground besides Lena and big bear. Big bear saw that one of the tall trees was missing a lot of bark.

The bark was all black, Big Bear took a closer look and noticed that there was a big buck rub.

"What are you looking at on that tree?"

"There's a buck rub over here on the tree."

"What's a buck rub?"

"It's when a male deer takes its antlers and rubs its antlers against the tree knocking off the bark and leaving a mark in the tree."

Thank you for explaining that to me. Alright now let's continue to go on with the hunt. You shouldn't rush the hunt.

I'm not going to rush it, Big Bear and Lena walked along slowly. You have to be careful not to step on any branches and make any kind of noise that would spook the deer.

Let me take the shot when you see the deer. No, this time I'm going to take the shot.

"Are you sure?"

"Yes."

"Is there any noise that you can make that will attract the deer any faster?"

"No," there's not.

We'll just have to walk around here until we come upon a deer. Let's keep quiet, one hour later big bear heard a rustling around behind a tall green bush. There were a few tall oak trees growing around the tall green bush.

He heard another rustling und, suddenly he saw, a big four-point buck. His antlers were on the small side, he had a heavy body. It was a nice size deer, it put its head down and began to munch on me grass. Suddenly it's ears perched up.

It kept on looking to the left and right. But stayed there for a while. It gave Big Bear just enough time to draw back his bow, his hand was shaking, but he let the arrow go anyway.

The arrow flew straight and hit the buck right behind the left shoulder, it ran a ways and collapsed onto its side.

"That was a good shot."

"How long do you think it's going to take for you to track down the deer?"

"It all depends on how far the deer has gone, it's no big deal I'm going to track it down and we'll be back on our way."

Now let me finish tracking this deer. Big Bear followed in the path of the deer. There was a blood trail leading him right to where the deer had fallen.

Another ten yards and came upon the deer. Its fur was a light brown color, it had me dark spots on top of its back.

It's antlers on the left side were kind of worn down. It's one hoof had a crack in it. It looked like it had been infected for a long time. Oh, what a nice-looking deer big bear.

> Could I shoot the next deer that we hunt?

> Sure, you can.

Big Bear quickly pulled out his sharp knife out of the sheath. He began to cut up the deer.

He separated the fur from the meat. He cut off me meat and continued on skinning the deer.

Once he got started it didn't take him very long to finish skinning it, help me to place the meat inside the meat bag.

Let's take all the meat that we can carry along with us, I'm going to leave the deer here.

"Why don't we have to leave it behind?"

"Because it's too big for us to carry with us."

"Help me to finish packing up the meat bag, Big Bear"

"How long do you think this meat is going to last us, it all depends on how much of the meat that we consume each day."

I eat more than you do, after a while they were finished packing up the meat bag. The meat bag was bulging, it couldn't hold anymore meat.

Big Bear swung the meat bag over his shoulder, his hands were all bloody and was his knife.

The blood was dried onto the blade of his knife, Big Bear mentioned to Lena that he wanted her to help me to find a nearby creek.

They kept on walking along, they on came upon a small slow flowing creek. There was a lot of green grass growing around the creek.

Big Bear took out his knife again and placed it in the creek. The creek water felt cold.

He took his knife and ran it through the grass to get the remaining blood off of it. He rubbed his two hands together under the water and the remaining blood came off of his hands.

He was glad to finally get the blood off of his hands, he had strong hands. His hands were getting too cold he pulled his hands out of the creek.

He happened to look down into the creek again and saw a crayfish scurrying around under the water. The crayfish was a bluish color and had small pinchers.

He only saw one crayfish, Lena watched from a far. She didn't want to get near the creek, Big Bear stood up, his both hands were cold.

It rubbed his hands together and it made them warm up. Big Bear took Lena's left hand and helped her to cross the creek she almost tripped over a slippery rock.

The bank of the creek was muddy and there were a lot of tree roots sticking out the side of the creek bank. Which made it difficult to climb over the bank of the creek.

Big bear and Lena slowly climbed over the creek bank, the area right ahead of them was thick with sticker bushes.

There were long sharp thorns on the end of the sticker bushes. The bushes were a bright green color, there were me rocks around the bushes.

The rocks were easy to avoid. Big Bear was glad that there were no boulders in the way that he would have to climb.

The ground was relatively flat; in many places the ground was very uneven. It was difficult to walk over the uneven areas. Lena almost slipped over a small branch that was laying on the ground.

Her ankle has got caught on the small branch. But Big Bear helped her over the branch.

The weight of the meat bag was beginning to make his left shoulder ache, Lena and big bear kept on walking. They walked through me tall grass again.

They came out into the open again, Lena was feeling tired. She sat down on a boulder and took me time to catch her breath.

She was carrying a meat bag over her right shoulder; Big Bear was beginning to feel the strain from carrying the heavy meat bag. He sat down on the brown tree stump.

Chapter 14: The Dream

Lena looked over at Big Bear and said I didn't think that the meat would be heavy. I'm stronger than you and I'm having difficulty holding up the meat bag.

I'm going to put down the meat bag and relax my muscles for a while. I feel tired. I'm sure you'll feel better once you eat something.

How about if you stay here Big Bear and I go gather me wood? That would be okay. Lena got up and walked into the woods. She walked through me mud and the ground was slippery.

However, she didn't slip. She just kept on walking. There was a sticker bush, it was in the way of Lena.

Lena slowly took her time and avoided the sticker bush, the sticker bush had long sharp thorns on it. She stepped over a large rock.

The wind began to blow; it was blowing at eight miles per hour. The wind was blowing in from the south, Lena happened to look up and noticed that the sky was turning gray.

A few clouds were moving slowly through the gray sky, the clouds reminded Lena of rain clouds.

The clouds were like puff balls, as she was looking up a flock of geese flew by. The one goose was missing a few feathers from its left wing. Lena looked back ahead again and kept on looking for me wood.

There was pine tree off to the right and a tall oak tree over to the left. There were me small branches just underneath the pine tree.

The branches looked like they had been there for a while, there was me green moss forming on the branches. The branches were thin, but this made them good for building a fire. Lena was feeling kind of cold.

Her body was shivering. However, she just ignored it. Lena thought I hope we aren't going to have another bad rainstorm.

She picked up as much wood as she could carry. Her arms were kind of weak, but she was still able to carry the branches. She quickly walked back the way she came, she almost got lost but continued on anyway. She walked through me tall yellow grass.

There was a large ants nest that was in the center of the tall yellow grass, there were a bunch of black ants crawling around every which way.

Lena ignored the ants nest and stepped right through it. She knocked over the ant's nest and the ants became increasingly irritated and went running all around Lena.

Lena just kicked the dirt, and it made the ants going flying out of her way. As she was walking along she heard a loud boom that came from the sky. At first it scared her, then she ignored it.

She heard it again, this time the loud boom from the sky seemed like it was much closer than the last boom. Lena thought that this was just the space people trying to play games with her and she didn't turn around and look behind her. She just, went on, as she walked along. A small rock hit her in the back.

It made her back hurt bad, that it almost caused her to collapse. Somehow she was able to regain her strength once again. He walked on until she reached the opening again. Big Bear was sitting on an old log.

He didn't look very happy though. What's the matter Big Bear? I heard another noise, and I was worried that the space people had took you away. No, I'm doing alright, but I'm tired that I feel like I'm going to collapse.

"What do you need?"

"I think I just need to sit down for a while, right now I feel I like I'm going to fall over."

I hope that you will go sit down. I'm going to go sit down right now, let me put the branches down here and I'll go sit down.

Lena carefully placed the branches down. She went over and sat down on the large tree root. She leaned back against the tree and almost fell asleep. Her head just like fell backwards.

Big Bear saw this and said Lena, you certainly don't look okay. Now tell me the truth and no lies. I was telling you nothing but the truth Big Bear.

Like I said I just feel tired from the hunt. Would you like to go on another hunt Big Bear? No and why would you ask me that Lena? I really don't know Big Bear. Lena let me get a fire started. Big Bear rubbed two sticks together and after a while they caught fire. me gray smoke came up from the sticks. There was me tinder on the ground.

The fire quickly began to get larger, now the fire was a good size. Lena moved closer to the fire; her hands were as cold as ice. She rubbed her hands together to warm them up, although her hands were severely chapped and were on the verge of bleeding.

She had to rub them together. Her hands got warm and her whole body was now beginning to warm up. She felt a calming sensation come over her. Lena looked at him and said I think we should start the journey back to the tee pee, why's that? I'm afraid that the space people are going to see us. No, I'm sure that we're safe.

He carefully handed his pair of binoculars to her, and she said thank you, why don't you take a look up in the sky and look for me spaceships. I will, Lena carefully looked in the sky, she didn't see anything, she gave the binoculars back to him. Suddenly a coyote came running past them.

It was chasing after a field mouse. But the mouse was not quick enough to get away, the coyote quickly caught the mouse in its mouth. Suddenly the wind began to blow; it was blowing at five miles per hour. It was seventy-eight degrees outside, and it was a beautiful sunny day. Big Bear sat down in the green grass and me ants crawled up and over his left leg.

This didn't bother him at all because he is not afraid of insects. Big Bear brought up his binoculars again and this time looked down at the valley below, he saw two other Indians riding on horseback. These Indians didn't look familiar to him; they might even be an enemy tribe. Big Bear was relaxed that he began to fall asleep, he immediately went into a dream, he dreamt about a white buffalo.

Him and a few other Indians were hunting buffalo when they saw the white buffalo. The white buffalo looked like it had been in a few brawls with the other buffalo in the herd. Its right horn had a few scratch marks on it, it's left horn was broken in half. It must have been broken a few years ago.

There were ten buffalo in the herd, and there were three baby buffalo, the three baby buffalos had dark brown hide. One of the baby buffalo was smaller than the other two buffalo and it walked slower than the rest of the buffalo. The mother buffalo was beside the three-baby buffalo; she was making sure that no predators were going to get to her babies.

One of the large male buffalos got too close to her and she slammed into the buffalo, with much force that the buffalo almost lost its footing and just about fell over. The buffalo just shook off the body slam and continued on its way.

The mother buffalo began to snort at another buffalo that was getting to close to her babies. The sky was clear and there was no cloud in the sky, the sun was out over the mountains, it was a nice seventy-five degrees outside. The valley was wide open, and there were no trees in sight for a few miles.

The ground was covered in green grasses, the ground was nice and flat and in me places the grass was slippery in me places due to yesterday's rainstorm. Big Bear was still in the dream, he usually doesn't dream very long, but on this particular day he had a long dream.

The other Indians that were with him took out their long bows and began to take aim at one of the Bulls. The three other Indians were pulling back the strings and slowly let go the arrows struck the bull buffalo right behind its left shoulder.

All of a sudden Big Bear looked over at the Indian that was standing off to his right was Keeko, he couldn't believe it, but he realized that he missed his brother much that he was dreaming about him. Keeko had war paint on his face and had a smile on his face.

Keeko and the other Indians ran after the buffalo, it took them awhile to finally chase it down and the buffalo fell down onto its left side. You could clearly see where the arrows had hit him. The white buffalo ran away to a safe distance between it and the Indians, it watched as the three Indians slowly walked up to the buffalo that was lying on the ground.

The buffalo had died from its injuries, the three Indians unsheathed there knifes and began to cut up the buffalo and take it back to the tribe. It took the Indians three hours to get the buffalo cut up and put the meat into the leather meat bags and they threw the meat bags over their shoulders and began to head back to their tribe.

The white buffalo didn't seem like it was afraid of the Indians, one of the Indians looked at Keeko and said to him.

That white buffalo is a shape shifter, which means that he can change into any he wants for a short while. Keeko said that's very interesting, what else do you know about shape shifters chief?

I don't know any more about the shape shifters, but if you want to I can ask the elder of the tribe and he can tell you more the shape shifters. Did you know that Big Bear is my brother, no I didn't know that, and he's right behind us.

Keeko turned around and was going to talk to big bear, but all of a sudden he woke up, but he didn't want the dream to be over.

Once he was awake he looked off to his left and saw that Lena was lying their next to him. She was sleeping, and her left arm was twitching.

He closed his eyes again and was hoping he would go back into the dream, but nothing happened. He decided to nudge Lena awake.

She looked at him and said why are you waking me up? I woke you up because I wanted to tell you that I had a dream about my brother Keeko, oh that's good, however I suddenly awoke and left the dream.

I hope you have another dream on, I really beginning to miss Keeko, I wish those space people would give me back my brother. I hope that they do, and on. How did it feel to lie flat on the grassy ground, it felt great.

I could feel the energy coming from Mother Earth and I could hear her talking to me.

"What did the Mother Earth say to you?"

"She said that I would be seeing my brother on, I shouldn't be worrying about the space people."

Chapter 15: Fight Back

It was now late in the evening and the sun was beginning to go down, there was a beautiful sunset. There was orange and the color red in the sunset.

Big Bear couldn't believe that it was night already, Lena pointed at the sunset and remarked to him that the sunset was the most beautiful sunset that she had seen in a while.

Big Bear accidentally dropped his binoculars on the ground, he quickly picked them up.

He looked down at the valley but couldn't see much because it was getting dark outside.

Suddenly they heard a loud rumbling sound, they both looked around but didn't see anything out of the ordinary. They looked behind them and saw that there was an old, rotted tree that had just collapsed.

The tree was very large, all of the bark had fallen off of it. There were a few small holes in the tree from woodpeckers.

The tree was missing a lot of its branches. It was an oak tree and looked like it had me kind of tree disease. Then suddenly they heard another crashing noise. They both immediately stood up and looked in every direction.

Big Bear happened to wander into the woods and noticed that there was a strange gray and silver spaceship hovering tree top level, it had a few windows and a strange looking latched door. There were blue lights on the sides of the spaceship.

The spaceship was hovering along at a slow speed, it seemed like the space people were looking for someone or something.

Lena grabbed a hold of his shoulder and said see I told you that we weren't safe from the space people.

Now because you didn't listen to me, the space people are now going to take us away, no, I don't believe that they are here for us.

"Why not?"

"I think that are looking for something besides us."

The spacecraft was silver and was reflecting the light off of itself, he hovered along slowly and stayed at tree top level.

Not sure what to do they both stayed still and observed the spacecraft, blue lights began to light up on both sides of the spacecraft.

There were two blue lights on either side of the spacecraft, the lights were bright that they were almost blinding if looked at too long.

Big Bear was wondering if the spacecraft was going to stay there awhile or just quickly take off.

On the one side of the spacecraft, it was black and looked like it had caught fire and turned black.

There was one small window at the front of the spacecraft, he couldn't see anything going on inside of the spacecraft.

The spacecraft wasn't very loud and in one second the spacecraft's engines turned on and it took off straight up into the sky, within a minute it was out of sight.

Big bear couldn't believe how fast it was, he thought to himself I don't know how I'm going to destroy the spacecraft and get my brother back.

Lena said don't worry he'll be back on; you must have told me that like fifty or more times and still he's not back. I'm going to have to find me good firepower to stop the spacecraft.

"Where are you going to go to find powerful weapons like that?"

> "I have a few white men for friends, and they know of a place where there's plenty of fire power."

It'll take me three days just to get there from here, I think that we need to get two horses to ride instead of doing all this walking.

Besides that, my little feet are getting painful from the hundreds of miles that I have walked. My feet are kind of sore to, but I keep going on.

I'm not trying to make excuses but somedays my feet really hurt, especially if I accidentally get a stone stuck in my shoe.

I thought that we were going to go home instead of going to your friend's armory. I have grown tired of these space people that I want to get after them and take back what's mine from them.

They have my brother; they aren't returning him back to me and that really has me angry and ready to fight back.

The afternoon went by very slowly and Lena was getting hungry Big Bear helped her to start a fire. It didn't take him long to start a fire, he had collected a bunch of small branches for the fire.

The temperature was beginning to rise, and this caused him to get hot and take off his shirt. Sweat was already pouring down his cheeks, he walked over into the shade and sat down in the green grass, although he kept on thinking about what the space people were doing to his brother.

With anger he picked up a stick and began to whack the bushes that were right in front of him. After a few minutes of doing that he got tired of it and threw the stick into the woods.

Lena kept a watchful eye on him, she was getting concerned with the way he was acting. She thought that he was going crazy, but she kept her thoughts to herself and never asked him what he was doing.

She sat down on a tree stump just a few yards away from Big Bear. She let out a yawn and looked up into the sky, she saw a big white fluffy cloud that reminded her of a rabbit.

She kept staring at the cloud and the cloud eventually moved on through the sky.

Lena took a small piece of meat and put over it on a stick and placed it in fire, it didn't take much time for the piece of meat to get blackened on one side.

She likes her meat well done and doesn't like to eat raw meat, he came walking over closer to Lena and asked her.

"Are you hungry?"

"Yes," I'm very hungry, my stomach keeps on grumbling.

"Would you like me to run your stomach for you?"

"No," thanks

I should be okay after I eat something, alright for you then.

"Aren't you hungry though?"

"No!" I have one thing on mind, and it won't leave my mind.

"What's on your mind?"

"I don't really want to talk about it because I'm angry about it, you know it's not well to hold in all that anger."

It may cause you to go out of your mind, I'm not going to go out of my mind anytime on. I'll figure it out oner than later.

I can tell that you want to leave me alone for the rest of the afternoon. I'll just mind my own business and not talk to you for a while today. He said OKAY and threw his arms up in the air and walked away from the campfire and took a short walk in the woods until he cooled down.

His body was tense that his muscles felt like they were locking up, he ignored the feeling. He didn't look where he was walking, and he tripped over a small stick.

He landed down and face planted right on his face, he let out a moan and could barely even get up.

He had to lay there until he could get all of strength back and get up, he looked up into the sky and saw that it was all blue sky.

There weren't many clouds in the sky. He let out another moan because his left shoulder was aching, he blacked out.

Lena got concerned because he hadn't come back after an hour, she took the piece of meat and ate it with one mouth full.

She quickly ran into the woods and didn't seem him; she began to grow even more nervous that something happened to him.

Maybe the space people have taken him away, her mind always thinks the worst for me reason.

She happened to look down and a few feet in front of her and she saw that he was laying on the ground. He appeared to be asleep, she bent down and put her hand on his left shoulder.

But he never woke up, she grew more worried about him, she loudly called his name and still no answer.

She checked for a pulse on his left wrist, there still was a pulse, she felt his forehead and it was sweaty.

She couldn't lift him, she had to sit with him, she tried to open his eyes, but they remained closed.

He began to twitch, and it scared her. So much that she moved further away from him, then as on as he began twitching he stopped.

His body went back to resting, big bear had went into a dream. He dreamt about the space people and that he was fighting with one of the space people.

He had a six-shooter pistol in his hand, and he shot one of the space people in the chest. The spacecraft slowly fell down to the ground in front of him, and Lena was in his dream. He dreamt that Lena was by his side trying to help him to kill the remainder of the space people.

She had a bow and arrow and was shooting flaming arrows at the space people, there were five space people.

His brother was on an old bar chair and was tied up to the chair and he had a sad look on his face.

"Are you here to rescue me?"

"Yes"

Then another one of the space people fell over dead after getting hit in the chest by a flaming arrow.

His friend was standing directly off to his left side, and he had a long rifle and was firing at the space people, now all the space people that were standing all around the chair in front of the chair that his brother was sitting in.

Lena began to cry because she wasn't sure that he was going to ever wake up again.

One tear ran down her left cheek, she wiped it off with her right hand, she tried to shake Big Bear awake.

But it didn't help, and he still didn't wake up. He remained sleeping and was still breathing, the space people seemed like they were making it too easy for him to get his brother back from them.

One of the space people was shaking and bleeding from the gunshot wound. Big Bear saw a tall space creature that came up behind where his brother was sitting and ripped the rope off of his hands and took him by the left hand and took him away, this creature was all green and had a long tail, it had a lot of sharp teeth and was quick when it walked.

It walked on two legs just like a man, but it was twice as strong as the rest of the space people. The creature had very angry look on its face, it must have been seven feet tall or taller.

It had large muscular arms and hands, its nails were very long and sharp. The creature and his brother disappeared, he said to everyone that was next to him to follow after the creature and his brother.

Suddenly the creature turned around and stared right into big bears eye, and he let a warning roar and roared again and when he did Big Bears friend shot him right in the chest with his muzzle loader, the smoke cleared. The creature was still there looking at the three of them.

Then Big Bear fired off his six shooter and hit the creature right in the center of his chest, the bullet did nothing but make the creature angrier.

The creature let out a roar and grabbed a hold of his brother again and began to run in the opposite direction.

They chased after him and he could run twice as fast as they could, it took them awhile to catch up to him.

Then the creature and his brother disappeared, and this really frustrated him. Lena opened up her canteen and poured water all over his face, this instantly made him jump up almost stepping on her left foot, now I see that you're awake again and are able to think and be yourself once more. It still seems like you have an attitude.

I have a because I saw my brother in another dream, and a strange terrifying creature took my brother away and I didn't see him again.

"Was I in your dream?"

"Yes," and you were right beside me shooting at the space people. In my dream I killed all the space people.

"Who else was in your dream?"

"My friend McGhee"

"What was he doing?"

"He was shooting at the space people too."

"How long has it been since you have seen McGhee?"

I haven't seen him for more than a year, I feel like I'm full of energy. I can't sit still and calm down, perhaps I ate too much red meat.

No, you just got yourself in a panic attack and you'll have to wait until your panic attack is over and you can relax.

"What are you trying to say?"

"I'm saying that I'm the leader here, if you want to be the leader, then start leading."

You haven't been very nice to me these past few days, and I know you're going to say that your just angry and that's why you're grumpy, I'm getting tired of hearing you argue with me.

"Do you want me to leave you alone then?"

"No," I just wish you would stop arguing with me, it's my life and I know how the world works.

"Why don't you go lay down and take a nap for the rest of the afternoon?"

I think that I'm going to do that, okay I hope when you wake up again you will have calmed down and act more relaxed.

I'm sure that I will, I hope I go back into my dream; I hope you do too, now get me rest.

"What are you going to do while I rest?"

"I'm going to take a short walk down to the creek and fill up my canteen and maybe pick me wild berries. "

Don't worry I'll be back on to check on you, I'm still kind of scared of what just happened you.

"I'll be okay for the rest of the afternoon."

"How do you know that?"

The good Earth spirits are watching over me. I'm just afraid that you're going to have a heart attack and pass away while I'm away, I can promise you that's not going to happen to me.

My body is good and strong yet, I hope that you don't black out again. I won't, I just black out every so often.

"What you get black outs often?"

"You didn't tell me about that."

I'm going to take you to the local Medicine Man and have him take a good look at you. I don't need his help; I would prefer for him just to leave me alone.

I think we should travel to the medicine man's teepee tonight, just let it go. Let's lay down and go to sleep.

Tomorrow we'll go straight to McGhees house and then from there we'll go to the armory and get ready to fight the space people.

Chapter 16: Battle

I’m not even tired, you still have to rest for the next day. If you stay up all night tonight, you won't have any energy for the long journey ahead. I’ll go to sleep as on as I feel tired.

I’m going to sleep awhile and be ready for tomorrow. I’ll go to sleep on; you keep on saying that, but you still aren't laying down. I’ll lay down next to you on.

While he was on his back he looked up into the sky and thought to himself, I’m sure the space people are just flying around up there in their spacecraft and don't have a care in the world.

He thought on about how he was going to take out all the space people and finally get his brother back.

He thought to himself it's not going to be easy to kill that alien creature. He began to fall into a deep sleep and, everything went black. He was asleep, Lena was still awake and kept on rolling on her right and left sides.

She couldn't get comfortable sleeping on the hard ground, she decided to lay on her stomach. Then she got a stomachache, she couldn't keep her eyes closed.

Her eyes were feeling tired, she was still very restless. While she was laying down a small lizard came crawling and crawled over her body.

She screamed out and said get off of me you crazy lizard. But Big Bear just kept on sleeping and didn't hear Lena yell.

Lena took a few deep breaths and calmed down. She still couldn't fall asleep; with the light of the moon, she could see around the woods well.

She decided to take a walk around, there was a green bush that had beautiful white flowers on them.

She picked one of the flowers and put it up to her nose, but there was no fragrance coming from the flower.

Then she picked another white flower and put it behind her left ear, this made her feel pretty.

Suddenly she got a bad cramp in her ankle, and this caused her to fall to the ground in pain.

She was now on her back; she reached down and began to rub her ankle. She let out a moan and said to herself why do I always get such bad cramps.

She figured that she just wasn't drinking enough water and that's why her joints were locking up and hurting.

She got a small scratch on her ankle, but it was nothing to be concerned about. She brushed herself off and got up and continued on her walk, it was almost a full moon this night.

She thought about doing her traditional moon dance that her great grandmother taught her how to do.

The memory of her great grandmother came into her head. She thought that her mind was playing tricks on her, she just ignored the thoughts and walked further into the woods.

She heard a strange noise and couldn't identify it or which direction that it was coming from.

She looked to her right and left and even behind her but there was nothing there, she thought to herself what if a spacecraft is watching me.

She walked over to a tall pine tree and sat down beneath its large branches. She hoped that if something was following her that it wouldn't see her sitting by the tree.

She began to shiver because it was cold outside, she thought about going back to where big bear was sleeping and sleep next to the fire.

She thought maybe I should go back to big bear instead of being out here alone. Suddenly a beam of light came up above her and stayed there for a while she didn't know what to do or what was going on.

She decided to stay still and not move, this would later prove to be a very bad decision and she would ultimately pay the price.

Two space people came down from the spacecraft that was hovering tree top level, one of the space people grabbed her and took her up into the spacecraft.

She tried to scream and fight her way out of the space people's hands but was stuck.

The space people tied her down and threw some kind of jelly like substance over her face and body.

She continued to scream out, this didn't seem to do anything to help so she stopped. She looked down at her feet and two space people were standing there, they had no kind of expression on their faces.

They were five-foot-tall, and their bodies were all gray and they had big oval shaped eyes.

One of them came up on her left side and grabbed onto her left arm, she let out a scream then calmed down. She wasn't sure what was going to happen next to her.

The night went by slowly and the next morning the sun came up over the great mountains.

Big Bear was feeling good and refreshed this morning, he heard me birds chirping off to the left of him. He looked to his right expecting that Lena was going to be laying there.

She wasn't this immediately made him think the worst. Off in the distance he saw a doe walking along with its young fawn standing next to her.

The doe's ears went up and she looked around, suddenly something had spooked her. The doe and her baby ran away deep into the woods.

He happened to hear something rustling around in a nearby thicket that was many feet away. He was thinking to himself I bet those space people took Lena last night.

He thought on wherever the space people are I'm going to go after them and stop them from going on.

Nearby there was a little cave, there were a few little trees that were growing around the opening of the cave.

The fire was still burning, he didn't take the time to put it out. He was too busy worrying about where Lena had gone, he quickly darted into the cave and hid

He peaked around the tree and kept watch on the thicket where he kept on hearing the rustling und. To his great horror it was the green alien creature that he had saw in his dream.

The creature was seven feet tall and had a rather long tail that slide along the ground while he walked along.

The creature was walking along slowly, it seemed like he was looking for someone or something.

The creature didn't look over in his direction, he was glad that the creature didn't spot him. The creature bent down and began to dig into the ground.

It lifted up its head and began to smell the air. Its nostrils were flaring, its eyes were staring straight ahead.

It kept a watchful eye on the fire, the fire seemed like it disturbed him. He walked over towards the fire and once again bent down and dug into the dirt.

He picked up a stick and a threw it into the fire, it was like he was experimenting and seeing how life was like on earth.

His green eyes were fully opened, he was aware of his surroundings. Then the creature stood back up and kicked the dirt right in front of the fire.

The dirt went into the fire and put it out. The creature didn't like the fire and seemed to be relieved after the fire was out.

A cool wind blew it from the East, the creature continued to explore the area. A hawk was flying overhead, the creature looked up in the sky and kept watch on the hawk.

A few feet away from the creature was a big rattle snake, it began to rattle its tail and began to slither through the grass, towards the creature.

The creature didn't know that the snake was there and kept on walking around, the snake struck the creature on its ankle.

The creature barely even felt the bite and reached down and picked up the snake and crushed it in its claws. Then ripped its head off and threw the snakes lifeless body on the ground.

The creature let out a roar and looked off to its left side and began to stare. Big Bear was terrified, that his body was beginning to shake, his palms were getting all sweaty, and sweat began to run down his forehead.

He was going to pull out his rag and wipe off his forehead but was too afraid to move or thought that he was going to be sighted by the creature and get attacked by the creature.

The creature didn't stop starring until a few minutes went by, he must have heard something and turned his head towards the other way.

Big Bear looked around the inside of the cave and he found a rock that had a sharp edge on it.

He was thinking about throwing it at the creature, then went on to think we'll I better not. He's probably twice as strong as I am and will try to kill me if I hit him with a rock.

He thought that it would be best for him to just wait awhile until the creature left and then he would be safe once again.

Big bear really wanted to fight the creature but knew that he should wait, until he has more powerful weapons before he fights the creature.

He took out his binoculars and looked down at the valley and he saw a cowboy and an Indian chief on horseback.

The cowboy had a rifle in his hand and was aiming it up in the direction of the creature.

He didn't recognize who the Indian chief might have been. He was wearing a big head dress with a few hawk feathers coming out of it.

The horse that he was on was all black and had a few white spots on his back. The Indian chief was riding the horse barebacked, the cowboy was riding with a saddle.

He saw that the cowboy went to reach into his pocket for me kind of device that looked like a scope.

He attached it to the top rail of the rifle and looked into the sight and took a shot, the bullet came only a few feet away from the creatures foot.

The creature jumped up and looked over in their direction and let out a warning growl, it began to walk in their direction.

Neither the cowboy nor the Indian chief moved away from their Positions. The cowboy quickly reloaded his rifle and looked back into the sight.

This time he shot and hit the creature in its abdomen, it did nothing to the creature.

It just made it angrier, and it kept on walking towards them. It was now a few yards away from them, then it began to run at them.

Both the cowboy and the Indian chief began to run the other way, the creature leaped up into the air and came down on the Indian chief. The horse and the Indian chief fell down.

The creature opened its mouth which had rows of sharp teeth and bit into the horse's neck killing it instantly.

The Indian chief couldn't run away quick enough from the creature, the creature chased him down and tried to bite his left arm.

The Indian chief was now fighting for his life, he kept on rolling around on the ground trying to fight off the creature. It was no match for the creature who was twice as strong as a man.

The creature got up off of the Indian chief and punched him in the center of his chest.

The Indian chief screamed out go get out of here, while you still can and fell over onto his back.

Blood came flowing out his mouth, he collapsed onto the ground and his body remained motionless

The creature left him and began to run after the cowboy, the cowboy had his horse running as fast as it could. He couldn't believe his eyes and a tear began to run down from his eye.

He felt bad for the death of the Indian chief. He looked back in his binoculars, he saw that the creature was still chasing the cowboy and that the creature almost caught up with him.

The creature got right up next to the cowboy and tried to pull him off of the horse. The cowboy kicked the creature on its side making it lose its balance for just a moment, afterward he punched the creature in its jaw.

He just kept on trying to get the cowboy off of his horse, the horse had a terrified look on its face and suddenly fell down onto the ground from exhaustion.

The creature picked the cowboy up by his shirt and threw him down onto the ground, so hard that both his knees snapped in half and the cowboy screamed on and on.

This only made the creature angrier, and it was in a violent rage and its nostrils were flaring.

The cowboy must have been in much shock after his both legs were broken, the cowboy fell onto his back and stopped moving and was no longer breathing.

He thought this creature is strong and can easily kill a man or even a horse. After the dust settled, the creature bent down and looked at the dead body of the cowboy.

It took its hand and felt the neck of the cowboy and it let out a loud growl that could be heard for miles.

There was blood on the creature's mouth, and it didn't care. It looked up into the sky and walked around in a circle.

He wasn't sure what to think, he thought to himself I hope this creature goes back to where it came from.

His hands were beginning to cramp because he held up the binoculars for too long.

He took a break and put the binoculars down and took in a deep breath. After a few minutes he picked up the binoculars again and began to look through them. To his amazement the creature was still standing in the valley.

Suddenly the creature raised up both of its arms and bent down in a crouched position and remained there for a while.

The creature stopped looking into the sky and began to look left and right, then straight ahead.

The alien creature seemed like it was still irritated for a reason unknown to Big Bear, the creature began to dig a small hole where it was sitting.

It sat down in the small hole and a long snake tongue came out of the creatures mouth and remained hanging out

It's tongue went back in its mouth and the creature went to lay down, it must have sensed something and stood up and looked around once more.

Further away from the creature a small beaver was slowly walking along and there were several beavers in all.

This was odd because there was no river close to them to go to, he thought to himself I hope that the creature doesn't kill the three innocent beavers.

The beavers kept on walking on getting closer to the where the creature was, the creature stayed around where he had dug the small hole.

The creature kept on keeping a watchful eye out, within a few minutes the beavers were now just several yards away from the creature. The creature noticed them almost immediately and seemed to not be bothered by them.

The creature turned its head and had a curious look on its green face, it sat down and was waiting for the beavers to get closer.

The beavers saw him first and stopped and looked at the creature, the creature quickly stood up and slowly began to walk up to the beavers.

The one small beaver fled as the creature got near him, the other two beavers were wondering what this creature was.

The creature bent down and put its hand out and one of the beavers tried to bite his other hand.

The creature quickly pulled its hands back away from the beavers. The two beavers flapped their tails on the ground like they were warning the creature not to get any closer to them.

The creature stood up again and tried to kick the two beavers with his left foot, but the beavers dodged his kick and ran away the other way from the creature.

The creature seemed to be getting very impatient and sat down once more. It kept its left eye watching the ground and its right eye to look up into the sky. Suddenly a spacecraft came into sight overhead of the creature.

Blue lights lit up all around where the creature was sitting. The lights didn't seem to bother the creature he just remained sitting there.

A large door opened up and big bear was waiting for something else to come out of the door, but just me smoke was flowing out of the spacecraft. This seemed kind of odd to him, but he kept on thinking.

A massive light came down overhead of the creature and it seemed to relax the creature and it laid down. His eyes were almost shut, a small platform came down from the bottom of the spacecraft.

Two space people walked out of the spacecraft and down the platform. The creature seemed to have greeted them, and they gave him a hug back.

The space people looked at the body of the cowboy, the body of the Indian chief and showed no kind of remorse for what had happened.

The creature's eyes opened wide, and it roared once more. Both space people didn't seem to appreciate this, and they pulled him aside and wrapped a chain around his neck.

The creature almost fell to its knees, he could see that there was electric pulsating through the chain that was around his neck.

He thought to himself maybe this creature is there pet, or maybe just an experimental creature that they had created.

Both space people pulled the creature along by the chain that was around its neck.

Both space people and the creature got back into the spacecraft, but the spacecraft stayed hovering just a few feet off of the ground.

The spacecraft began to spin in a counterclockwise motion, then started over again but this time began to turn clockwise.

This went on for almost fifteen minutes, he couldn't believe his eyes. He had never saw a spacecraft spin around like this one was.

He was hoping that the door would reopen, and Lena would come walking out. But no such luck, a tear began to run down his cheek.

He used his hand and wiped away the tear, he couldn't believe that his wife was now gone too. He feared that she would never be back.

Suddenly the spacecraft took off straight up into the blue sky, it passed through one large puffy white cloud.

Within a matter of seconds, it was gone somewhere up in the sky. His heart was beating fast because he was nervous about what happened. He decided to lay down and get into a more relaxed mood.

While he was laying down a beautiful yellow butterfly flew past his head and slowly flapped its long wings.

This put a smile on his face, he thought to himself things must not be that bad. I'm now safe and secure and won't have to worry much about the creature. After that day, while walking along a trail he discovered his wife's body.

He began to weep and began saying a prayer, after the prayer he took his wife's body back to his village and the villagers helped him bury his wife's body.

Into his later years, he would rarely journey far away from the village. He died of natural causes two years later.

www.ingramcontent.com/pod-product-compliance
Lightning Source LLC
LaVergne TN
LVHW091304150826
845673LV00006B/1536

* 9 7 9 8 8 2 0 3 8 8 8 8 0 *